MARGINAL ENEMIES

NORMAN BEAUPRÉ

The serious injury done to Gregor ... seemed to have made even his father recollect that Gregor was a member of the family, despite his present unfortunate and repulsive shape, and ought not to be treated as an enemy.

Metamorphosis by Franz Kafka

For Michael and Henning

CHAPTER ONE

Two men, both in their early fifties, one hunched over his empty cup of coffee, the other staring into space, both saying nothing, wait with tickets in their pockets for a performance of *Cabaret*. These two men from two different countries, two continents apart, sit in a Berlin bar after a long chat, the Paris Bar on *Kantstrasse* where everyone goes after a theater performance. Another man, a writer, watches them as they slowly get up from their table, nodding their heads in some sort of agreement to leave the premises, one following the other, both silent in their thoughts and words; they quietly go out the door, crossing the doorsill without paying too much attention to the inscription at their feet, *Passant Sois Modeme*. He sits there wondering. Wondering what if … what if these two gentlemen were to become the subject of his next writing. A novella, perhaps even a full-fledged novel. After all, a writer needs some kind of inspiration and he gets it wherever he can, sometimes in stranger places than this and usually when he least expects it. Why not write a novel about this? he asks himself in the meandering solitude of his mind. What a fascinating subject. Two men from two enemy countries during World War II meeting like this and talking about their memories as boys during this God-awful madness of a war. The writer just sits there intrigued by his thoughts. The waiter brings him the check; he takes some *mark* notes from his right pants pocket, selects one and places it on top of the check. He gets up, catches the mirror from the corner of his eye, looks into it and sees an empty table. He smiles. Then he slowly walks out, takes a left and fades into the bustling crowd.

Three years passed and the writing began; the matter had been stored like some shiny brass buttons in a cache of buttons clipped off many fabrics gotten too old, too faded, or plain worn out. Buttons are like life experiences, too good to throw away, often forgotten, but held in reserve, for someday they might be useful.

The writer came across one of his notebooks in which he kept his fleeting bursts of inspiration followed by thought-out notations. He found his notes from the Paris Bar and rummaged through them. He then sat down and began to work things through. He thought of the two men in that Berlin bar. They were not really old, but old enough to remember bits and pieces of the Second World War from a child's perspective. Then the idea of *enemy* hit him. From what perspective does one see the enemy? It always seems to be from the personal or the politically linked angle. Sometimes enemies are inherited from generation to generation, part of a tribal memory. When does it stop or does it ever? Are children enemies? Children of children? Must one always choose sides?

All these questions and more whirled in his head. He snapped out of his wondering and began to construct his story. He would model his two main characters after the two men he had come across at the Paris Bar three years before. He even saw them again in his mind's eye, their profiles forever frozen in the bar mirror. The inspiration for his story had finally fallen into place, much like the loose bits of colored glass that form a bright pattern in a kaleidoscope.

Two men. Two human beings brought together somehow by fate, somehow by circumstance. One a Berliner, the other a native New Englander. From different ethnic backgrounds, the fair-headed one of Teutonic origins with an Alsatian name; the other, dark-haired and full-faced, of a French background, a descendant of Norman low bourgeoisie, with a slight mixture of Native-American blood thanks to the errant ways of *coureur de bois*. No real reason why they should meet like this except for some fortuitous circumstance, just like the strings of puppets being pulled in deliberate and orchestrated ways by a hidden colossal puppeteer who makes the figures walk, dance, or even stumble.

The circumstances in this case are part of a scheme of things whereby the son of the Berliner is studying at the small university where the New Englander is teaching. By way of a first encounter where mutual attractions are at work, the arts, travel, languages, and a profound respect for learning become the subject matter for an initial conversation between student and teacher. Later, other conversations ensue which develop into further encounters, longer conversations, and eventually a meshing of ideas, tastes, feelings, and intuitive gestures that invite friendship. The younger man is fashioned with enough maturity and the older one retains a sufficient amount of youthfulness that the two are comfortable enough in their relationship to fully enjoy each other's company.

When the father visits his son prior to commencement, he is introduced to the teacher. The meeting leads to an invitation to Berlin. Fortunately, an upcoming sabbatical year gives the teacher the opportunity to spend a couple of weeks in the former capital with the father before going on to Paris, where the teacher plans to do research and writing. He is pursuing a mounting interest in the legend and artistic treatment of the Green Man in Gothic architecture that emerged from his previous research in and around the Île-de-France with a summer grant from the National Endowment for the Arts. That's when he discovered that the Green Man existed not only in France but in England and Germany as well. His very favorite is the Bamberg Green Man on the Rider's console, the one with the singular wild eyes peering through acanthus leaves. When the father suggests to the teacher that he visits Berlin and, at the same time, offers him to stay with him in his home on *Koenigsallee*, well, he jumps at the opportunity, keeping Bamberg at the back of his mind.

For both men, historical events are integrated parts of classroom discussion and assigned readings as well as bedside reading, but not deliberate parts of daily living and certainly not considered as main valued in judging character and national origins. Past history is thus a negligible factor in the developing friendship of these two men. The Berliner was early on introduced to art and medicine since his mother is an art historian and his father a doctor. The other man is from a working-class family in a neighborhood where a college graduate is definitely the exception. By a curious paradox that melds duty and meekness with sheer determination and prompting to be different, he pulls himself up from a world of shoe shops and cotton mills to become a sheepskin recipient. Things are easier for the Berliner, as both his father and mother experienced the world of academia and it is part of the family heritage. Thus, he progressively passes on from *gymnasium* to university as if it were a matter of course. For the New Englander, the academy was new territory, as yet uncharted by his family. It was not easy at all, but worth the effort by means of the good fortune of financial grants and loans.

For one man, Europe is real, a place where people live, where relatives and friends work, marry, raise a family and where life continues to be shared on a continent with a multitude of countries, some small, others larger. For the other man, Europe is an area in geography textbook, a chapter in a history book, a locale for a movie. Much like North America, Europe is not a home. Continents are geo-political locations; cities and towns where people live and die are much more real places. Besides, people are what stories are all about.

The writer now has the story straight. He allows himself the reconstruction of the long conversation he overheard between two men three years ago in Berlin. The Berliner and the New Englander. He had watched them in the mirror across the room without their noticing him. It was a small room, a bar where people mingled easily. The Paris Bar. Not an extraordinary place, but a cozy place where people liked to go. It had a good reputation with theatergoers. Even Stephen Spielberg, it was said, went here at one time.

Not that the writer was spying on the two men. But he couldn't help glancing, now and then, at their profiles and especially at their gesticulating hands as if he had become a witness to a surrealistic puppet show. The figures were in the mirror while the sounds of their voices came over his shoulders, a kind of bizarre reality much like the Velazquez painting, *The Maids of Honor.* The writer had gleaned enough information from the encounter between the Berliner and the New Englander to construct an entire story around their conversation at the Paris Bar. It had ripened in his creative mind, and now the matter of his new novel could be put down in writing. Finally, things came together. At last, the story could be told.

CHAPTER TWO

Two men. Once, two children. Two young boys living continents apart from one another, never anticipating that one day they would meet. Two boys who were at one time enemies according to the conventions of birth and citizenship at a time when the Third Reich goose-stepped its way into territories not its own. War was a kind of a game for the New Englander. Barely seven years old in the mid-forties, he lived with the notion that war was "over there" and in movies that depicted American and British fighters teaming up to wallop the daylights out of the German enemy. It was a time when Hitler was the devil incarnate, Mussolini, the bullish, fat-faced Italian fascist, and, later, the Japanese Hirohito and his prime-minister, Tojo, the arch-evil, slanted-eyed enemies in yet another far-away land, this one across the Pacific. What captivated the young New Englander, as he grew up, were the spy thrillers with the fiendish Gestapo spies, stereotypically wearing long black leather coats with silver skulls on their lapels. Those black and white movies seemed all the more stark in their reproduced locales with spine-chilling shots of dark and musty places where torture inevitably took place. All Germans were bad. Mussolini was bad because of his alliance with the Nazi regime, but the Italian people themselves were not bad. All Japanese were bad because they were Japs, and all Japs were out to get the American people. Besides, the word itself, *Jap*, had an ugly ring to it. *Jap! Japs!* Like the sound of a fiendish dog barking in the night. Furthermore, the young New Englander never thought of the Germans as individuals, but rather as a collectivity of evil men who masterminded evil plots to conquer people and their lands in a far-away place called Europe. Besides, weren't they the mortal enemies who had blasted their way through Europe just some thirty years before the start of the "Big One" in the late thirties? *NA-TTT-ZEE*—a name that hollows your insides much like the tolling of the knell. As for the German people, that was just words, a kind of a vague idea that simply streaked through the mind without leaving any significant traces. Besides, there were no American movies about the German people, no songs about them, no newsreels. Just Nazi propaganda.

The young New Englander's name was Gérard. Things were much clearer back then when Gérard was growing up. Everything was black and white. It was just like the movies. So many fathers, just like the young New Englander's dad, told youngsters growing up that things were that way: good and evil, right and wrong, the hero side and the villain side. The American way and the non-American way. The young Gérard never heard of boys and girls growing up with mothers and fathers in Germany. He only heard of men marching to the orders of darkly-mustachioed creatures wearing highly-polished boots and sometimes spectacles or monocles.

He never heard of Jews, either, except for Sam and Eliot, the Cohen brothers, one who owned a men's furnishing store, the other who, with a benign smile, operated a small grocery store where the finest of vegetables and fruits could be had. Of course there was the synagogue on Bacon Street whose gray exterior with gold Hebraic lettering melded in with the apartment houses where non-Jews lived. And then there was the question of the Jews as Christ-killers, but that reference was only made on Holy Saturday when the lighting of the fire and the blessing of the waters were done and the Easter celebration began with the ringing of the bells at the *Gloria*. At noontime, all fasting was over, and it was a time when even the Jews in Gérard's town celebrated Easter basket day with the Christians.

The Jews ate milk chocolate Easter bunnies just as the gentiles had partaken of their matzos because they liked them better than saltines.

The Jews, the Poles, the Irish, the French, the Armenians, and the Italians were all part of the fabric of the young New Englander's everyday life when he was growing up in his part of the world. Everything was in its place where it should be and people got along because they were in their places, too. The Irish neighborhood, the Jewish side of town, the Italian hill, and the Little Canada—all places where people belonged. As for the Poles and the Armenians, well, they didn't have a place of their own, but they blended in.

Even the Germans were in their place across the sea, but they had somehow gotten out of hand, hadn't they, by crossing over into other places where they didn't belong. Besides, they were bad and mean-looking. They had become the enemy because everyone said so, and American troops were going to straighten out this God-awful mess through sheer determination and, of course, moral and patriotic fortitude. Everyone knew that. Might makes right, and forces of the good conquer all. That was what they said. Yes, there were a few inconveniences, such as the tokens and ration stamps, the long lines, and the waiting. One couldn't buy tires and butter without going through some inconvenience. Shoes were hard to get, too. Like so many other families, Gérard's family observed the meatless, wheatless, and porkless days and thus carried out the conservation rules of the U.S. Food Administration. Sometimes Gérard heard the words *black market*, but that was a hushed-up word used by grownups. At times, the young boy wondered why certain families, especially the well-off Yankee families whose fathers and grandfathers ran businesses and sat on boards of directors, had easy access to goods. He found out later that was called privileges in a system that rewarded civil responsibility, especially one of longstanding heritage. Gérard soon learned that privileges and access to success and wealth worked hand in hand, and he was going to find out how this was done so that he could, one day, partake of the making of a bright future based on civil duty and all the privileges that went with it. Of course, he would have to learn and apply himself. His only worry was whether his dad could afford to pay for his education after high school. If he had the good fortune to go to high school. Some of his ethnic colleagues never had the chance to go to high school, much less college. After all, boys grew up to become young men who were expected to help provide for the family. That's the way it was. That is, if they didn't get killed at war.

While Gérard was growing up in his own part of the world, the German boy was part of a family of two children whose father was conscripted into the army and sent to Italy to take care of wounded and dying soldiers. It had not been easy for the father to get his credentials as a medical doctor in Germany, for as a young man in his mid to late twenties, he had very little money and after he got married, his young wife had to stay at home to take care of their first child. Even when he was studying at the university, he had experienced terrible hardships. He couldn't afford light and heat in his student quarters, a one-room apartment across the way from the university. In the wintertime, he often had to go and study in the U, the subway tunnels in Berlin, so that he could get enough light to read his textbooks while indulging in the comfort of the heat provided by the subway station. He managed; that's the only way he could attain his dream.

Besides, how could he break the chain? After all, both his grandfather and his father were doctors. He thought that times would get easier and the profession of physician would indeed afford him and his family the necessities of light, heat, adequate clothing, and a few luxury items, such as tobacco and Viennese pastries. He learned to sacrifice comfort and security in order to seek a brighter future where he envisioned a family life full of satisfaction and love.

The First World War had come and gone without his being personally touched by it. His grandfather had told him about the signing of the treaty of Versailles. His family, however, in spite of being a doctor's family, had suffered like so many others who found themselves under the heel of the punitive indemnities and reparations imposed by the newly formed League of Nations. Thirty-three billion dollars was arrived at as a minimum figure. Where in the world would defeated Germany get the money? From the worn-out pockets of the people? For years to come, they would pay. Widows, orphans, and displaced people and all. After all, they had been defeated. What did it matter if it turned out to be a war without victory? The enemy needed to be crushed, humiliated, said the conquering victims who cried out for indemnities. Enemies are enemies and those in the right insist on reparations. So it became an armistice of vengeance, a means of a fragile, arm's-length, political peace, but also a means of wallowing in self-righteousness while the ugly worms of hatred were eating their way through men's souls.

For the young Berliner, Morgen was his name, much of what was happening around him as he grew up was surrounded in silence by the line that's often used with youngsters: "you're too young to understand." All he understood was that his father was away in Italy doctoring soldiers. His mother had insisted that the father did not want to go; he was, as she so often repeated in a low voice, "a pacifist at heart." *Ein Pazifist*. Later, when Morgen could look up words in a dictionary, he found out that "pacifist" meant one who opposes war and even force to settle things. But why did Vater have to go where the war was? After all, the young boy reasoned, he's a doctor not a soldier.

There were now two children; a girl was born a year after Morgen's birth. It was nineteen forty-two. The boy was five going on six. His mother, everyone called her Lotte, decided to bring both children to a place in the countryside where her cousin lived. Far away from the turmoil of the large cities like Kassel and Munich, whose buildings and industries attracted the bombs of the enemy. Her cousin was a Dunkelntappen; her father had married Lotte's aunt on her mother's side. Both parents had died and had left the small family farm to their only child, Sophie, who had never stepped outside the confines of her farm. She was an upright woman, although headstrong, and a good worker. A bit dull, but dependable. Her parents had kept her home so much that eventually she quit school altogether. She had hardly any relatives, and none were known except for Lotte. Lotte wrote to her once or twice a year around the holidays. She rarely got anything back from Sophie, except once, when she had sent Lotte a get-well card even though Lotte had not been sick.

Lotte packed up some of her belongings, the children's clothes and some of their toys, and of course some books so that she could continue to teach them something about reading and writing while in exile. At least that's what she called it. Exile. Although she resisted bringing too many heavy objects, she could not resist the urge to take at least one oversized book on art history. After all, she told herself, we are not barbarians. The children thought they were going on an extended holiday and left Kassel with a happy heart. As they boarded the train, the boy noticed how the people he tried to meet with his glance were quick to lower their eyes; they seemed to be in a rush, for everyone walked with a hurrying step. Most people seemed to be leaving with a longing mixed with anxiety on their faces. To a child's eye and heart, these faces were not carefree faces; rather, they were mirrors of what appeared to be wrong with the way everyday living had become. Even the neighborhood had become strange and somewhat eerie to the young imaginative mind in the constant struggle to process what was going on.

Exactly what was going on? Morgen wondered. He could see that his mother had grown tense in appearance, curt in her answers to questions, uneasy in her manner of doing things, and troubled in her gaze. Grown-ups seemed worried all the time. Morgen realized more and more that they had become paradoxically distant in their communication with children while being overly protective of them. The child, of course, did not have all of the proper words at his disposal to verbalize his feelings, but, nevertheless, he felt them profoundly, like a baffled witness to a terrible event unfolding before his eyes. Morgen and his sister, Jenny, sensing that things were awry with the grownups, reflected in their own disposition and subdued behavior the lack of liveliness that now saddened people's faces and deadened their enthusiasm. All children seemed to be affected by this pall of robot-like comportment. It was as if the children had been dragged into the sullen temper of the times.

The whistles blew, the iron wheels started to turn, and the train ventured out of the station. Morgen, his sister, and their mother sat quietly in their compartment, number 12, as the city and its tall buildings began to disappear from sight. All that was left to see through the windows was the ever-increasing grayness of a cluster of geometric shapes. As the train picked up speed, the boy settled in his seat across from his mother and started to play with his toy soldiers. The mother was gently removing Jenny's hat when the door to the compartment opened, showing a gloved hand holding on to the handle. A man in his late fifties stood in the doorway and asked the mother if he could sit down with them. The woman answered with a detached yes.

He was a graying man with a handsome face. He wore a dark brown, checkered, woolen coat with a short cape attached to the collar that went to his elbows. He took off his hat and gloves and unbuttoned his coat, all the while under Morgen's intense observation. The man smiled at the boy and gently touched the blond head. The man then turned to the woman and introduced himself as Herr Spiegel. Morgen's mother smiled with a politeness ingrained since childhood. Morgen looked up at the visitor and started asking him questions. His mother tried to restrain him, telling him that the man could not be bothered by the intrusive questions from a boy he had never met. Herr Spiegel brushed aside her concerns with a slight wave of his right hand.

"Where are you going?" asked Morgen.

"I'm going to Austria," replied the man.

"Why?"

"Because it's home."

"Oh," said Morgen. "We're going away from home, we are. We're going—" and his mother stopped the conversation at this point.

She looked directly at the man and asked him which city he was returning to.

"Salzburg," he answered.

"Mozart's home," she said.

The man smiled widely. "I miss the mountains."

"But there are mountains here in Germany," she was quick to point out.

"Yes," he agreed, "but not like *sie Heimat*."

"But Germany is also your home," she said, "now that we are once again one people."

There was a long pause before the man gave his reply. A hint of disenchantment suddenly appeared in his mellow voice as he explained. "I know," he said. "I am pleased that the Führer has brought us together like one big family, but you see home is home and I must return to my daughter who is waiting for me."

"Oh, you have a daughter?"

"Yes," he said. "She's the only one I have left. When my wife died, I tried to keep what remained of the family together, my sons and my daughter. After the death of my two eldest sons, I felt that I was losing everything. One died in a hunting accident and the other, *ein Selbst. . .*" He could not finish the words.

After an uncomfortable pause, the man resumed his tale. "The youngest one is now in the Führer's army somewhere. I haven't heard from him for months ... not even a note ... no formal word from the *Reichswehr* either. It's very difficult waiting to hear from someone so close to you." Herr Spiegel sighed briefly. "I came here to Germany to try and connect with our newfound solidarity, but...." He stopped himself from going any further with this line of thought.

"I'm sure that your son will soon get in touch with you." The mother tried to offer comfort to the man.

"You are fortunate for your children are still too young to be conscripted," he replied. "They are with you."

"*Gott sie Dank!*" she quickly responded. Then she added in an unguarded moment, "One never knows how things will turn out."

The man avoided her eyes and sat there rubbing the nail of his left thumb with the fleshy cushion of his right thumb.

Morgen had not dared to utter a single word while his mother and the man were talking, but taking advantage of the lull in the conversation, he burst out saying, "Are you ever coming back?"

"Shush," said his mother.

"It's quite all right," the man responded, "I don't know, boy."

"Why don't you know?"

"Because grown-ups don't always know what's waiting for them."

"Why?"

"Because some people like to make rules for others to obey and although some people do not like to follow their rules, they learn that they don't have much choice."

"Why?"

"Because that's the way things are, I suppose." The man shook his head wearily. "We learn to trust children and they deserve our trust when they are very young, but as they grow up things change. Men tend to become their own worst enemy at times. When you have worms gnawing at your insides, well, they have to come out."

"I had worms once," the boy replied. "My mom made them come out."

"That's enough," the mother insisted.

"What's an enemy?" asked Morgen.

"Well, now," the man said. "That's a big question, one that I cannot fully answer. But I can tell you what a friend is."

"What is a friend?"

"A friend is like a bird you really like but don't capture, like a flower that you don't pull out, or even like a tree that you don't cut down. For, you see, they live as friends because you allow them to be themselves."

"I have friends," said Morgen.

"Yes, I know. Keep them that way."

"Do you have friends?" asked Morgen.

The man looked up at the woman and replied wistfully, "Nowadays, it's hard to tell."

The woman's glance darted to the window and remained there like icicles grafted on frozen glass. For a long time, only the brakes in the railway could be heard as the train sped its way east, for it appeared that words had run out for the occupants of compartment number 12. The family got off the train at Bamberg and said their goodbyes to the man, who was staying aboard. The boy asked if they were there, the place of their final destination, since he could not see any farmland in sight. The mother told him, reassuringly, that they still had some way to go, but that they would reach their destination before nightfall. They then boarded another train whose destination was southwest.

Meanwhile, in New England, Gérard was not going anywhere other than to the neighborhood grocery store, where his big dilemma was whether to spend the entire nickel his grandmother had given him for errands. Should he spend part of it on some penny candy in the glass showcase? Let's see, licorice, little marshmallow hot dogs, some Mary Janes, or a little pie-like fudge with a tiny metal spoon? Which one was it going to be? Once the choice was made, the old owner was relieved, though he still mumbled that these kids squandered his time with penny nonsense. But he had learned to swallow his disgruntlement a long time ago. After all, business was made up of dimes, nickels and even pennies, and these tykes would grow up to be customers.

Gérard had seldom been outside his own neighborhood. Once or twice he had accompanied his parents and sisters for a visit to his mother's relatives, not too far away. Like most children where he lived, life revolved pretty much around the neighborhood and the parish community. Neighbors were abundant and everyone knew one another. Generations upon generations had lived there bringing up their families. Families begat families, and the cycle of relatives intertwined with neighbors followed its endless path. Nothing ever seemed to change. Until the war broke out. Then, as in the earlier war, families were separated from their sons once more. The first war seemed distant now and only the memories of someone's uncle or grandfather who had waged war in the trenches remained. Like the faded browned photographs in a family scrapbook, the memories of the Kaiser's war were now but a diminished account of a terrible time.

Sons and daughters were brought up in the neighborhood; they were educated there and many followed in their parents' footsteps and found jobs in the local mills, jobs that required little formal education. Besides, training was easy to come by, with helpful relatives, friends, or neighbors. Thanks to the war effort, things were better now, financially speaking. Jobs were plentiful. More and more women got jobs; they became an active part of the war effort. Luxuries such as store-bought clothes, cars, owning one's home, and recreation outside the home that would have been considered foolish expectations during the ravaging years of the Great Depression were now becoming realities. The neighborhood that had been considered safe, comfortable and had filled everyone with a deep sense of belonging right along, the neighborhood not only continued to be that way, but, moreover, it now provided people with a feeling of anticipation and hope. War overseas provided this hope, a hope of a brighter future couched in success and immeasurable opportunities. It's strange, some people said, strange that it took a war to bring that which people only wished for before but which had never materialized.

When America joined forces with its European allies to stem the onslaught of the common enemy, a new force had erupted in American neighborhoods, the force of being on the right side, the other side from the enemy's side. After all, this was the Big One. Furthermore, the politicians liked to repeat, it was the strength of its own ingenuity as seen in its technological advances and industrial power that made America strong. It took downright goodness and American know-how integrally linked to a dyed-in-the-wool red-white-and-blue patriotism to foster a deep sense of duty both at home and abroad. Strength and duty, they said. Now here's two words that characterized neighborhoods like the one where the young New Englander lived.

When wives had to count their pennies and dimes as well as their tokens at the grocery store, it was out of patriotic duty. When husbands had to make do with used tires and economize on their fuel and use ration stamps, that was considered part of the war effort. When children waited in line with their parents in order to get a chance to buy shoes, that was to provide for the men and women who were serving their country. And when housewives had to spend time opening the capsule that contained the yellow coloring to mix it with the large blob of greasy margarine, that was as part of their duty to ration butter so that the fighting troops might eat sufficiently well. In spite of the rationing, the blackouts, the civil patrols, and the sacrifice of their young men, the neighborhoods not only survived, but they prospered. Faithful and reverential prayers were said every day to help protect the American troops and to inflict great harm on the common enemy, the Germans.

Gérard grew up within the bosom of such a neighborhood where not only were the patriotic ties secure, but the knowledge of joining a united effort to help overcome the power of evil was exhilarating. The newscasters, the singers, the writers of popular radio shows all proclaimed the patriotic fervor of those fighting for the cause of freedom. Movies illustrated magnificently the strength of character and the might of arms of those who fought for the American way. Movies concretized the enemy. In black and white. Movies also became the manifestation of individual hopes and the measure of success at joining forces in a collective dream of making the world a better place to live, free of all enemies. Gérard was part of this American dream. He was constantly encouraged to foster this resolve so he could grow up safe, secure, and ever on the right path.

Sometimes Gérard would accompany a relative or an older friend to the City Theater. On Saturday afternoon, for twelve cents each, he and his neighborhood friends could sit through an hour and a half of cowboys and Indians movies. The theater manager would also throw in a serial every Saturday, *Captain Marvel or The Black Commando*, among a variety of cliffhangers, so that the kids could talk about it all week long and beg their parents to please not let them miss the upcoming episode. How could you play at being the hero of a serial if you missed any part of it? Serials were part of every week, just like the weekly bath, weekly church, and weekly dressing up. Blood would curdle, eyes would pop out, and the heart would beat faster and faster every Saturday afternoon as the hero ended the week's episode in peril. Everyone knew of course that at the very end the hero would win and the enemy would be destroyed. They knew that stories always ended that way.

Roy Rogers, Gene Autry, Hopalong Cassidy, and the Red Ryder

with Little Beaver were actors in the great adventure of shooting the Indians who were constantly plotting to kill the good people. They had meanness stamped on their faces, those Indians did, and evil shone in their eyes. What the neighborhood boys liked about these movies was that there was no kissing in them, well, hardly any. Of course, Dale Evans was there and sometimes Gene Autry sang to a girl, but there was no real romancing. Why would men of the West, the authentic Americans of history tales, want to have anything to do with love and kissing, anyway? Gérard would go home after each movie and talk for hours with his friends about the perilous conclusion of the last episode of the serial, the way cowboys always rode their well-saddled horses while shooting with both hands at the Indians. Sometimes there were some evil white men, not the real enemy, though, but vicious guys who plotted against the hero. However, their character was revealed in their facial features. They were dirty, with a month's growth of beard, they had shifty eyes or scars on their faces that resembled ugly crusts on old stones or decayed wood.

As for the girls and mothers, they preferred love stories and musicals. Deanna Durbin, Bobby Breen, and the like. They especially liked movies that had tears and sad endings. Why, the boys always wondered, would anyone want to go to a movie to cry and watch people suffer? All that talking and hugging and kissing was far beyond the boys' grasp. Once, Gérard was taken to a theater by his aunt and uncle, to a movie the aunt especially wanted to see. It was called *To Each His Own*, and it was a movie that was hard for the boy to understand. He didn't understand the plot, nor could he make any sense of the dialogue (except for the war part), and when he asked his aunt to explain, she told him that it was a grown-up movie and that kids were not expected to understand everything. Why, the seven-year old asked, would anyone want to see a movie that was hard to understand and, furthermore, filled with mushy stuff?

"Because," the aunt had stated, "*just because*. And, besides it's so beautiful...." And then she added, "Didn't you feel anything for the mother who finds her lost son at the end?"

"No," the boy answered. "I didn't even know she had a son. She wasn't even married!"

The evening's entertainment had ended with the aunt and uncle buying Gérard a sundae at the ice cream parlor and talking about real-life things.

Meanwhile, on the other side of the ocean, Morgen had already spent the fall at the cousin's farm. There had been no *Oktoberfest* that year. However, they were preparing for the Christmas season with all of its snow activities and its rejoicing of carols, the Christmas *Stöllen* and gingerbread houses. And, most of all, there was to be the Christmas *crèche*. Yes, the *Kleinkinderbewahranstalt*. Much to the children's dismay, there was no crèche available. Cousin Sophie did not believe in such things and, since there were chores to be done, holiday or no holiday, had always quietly celebrated the holiday with a good meal on Christmas morning. What with German pancakes, the white veal sausage, the *Brötchen* with Dutch cheese and the *Streuselkuchen*, the meaning of Christmas, Cousin Sophie said, was really in the tummy.

With cautious diplomacy and a woman's way of mending things, Morgen's mother quietly assured her children that ways could be found to make a *crèche*. One had to be ingenious, she said, for ingenuity can overcome many obstacles. "What's ingenious?" asked Jenny, and Morgen responded, "It means putting your thinking cap on."

The mother had taught them how to think when they came face to face with a problem. She had knitted each of them a stocking cap, one bright red, the other yellow, and had told them that, regardless of any circumstance, when some good thinking needed to be done, one had to do it quietly and deliberately. Everyone could think and be creative. The stocking cap was there to help one think; the cap could not think by itself, of course, but once on the head, it had the power to produce ideas in the head, for it warmed the brain much like a hen who hatches her eggs. The mother knew that eventually the children would lose the magic of absorbing everything through their imagination without first sifting it through reason, but much like Father Nicholas and *das Elfenreich*, she enjoyed the old ways and encouraged the simpler times and ways that had lived before everything became demythologized.

So now the children got to thinking about making a *crèche*. It did not take too long before Jenny thought of something. "Why not make a *crèche* out of paper?" she asked.

Morgen responded by suggesting that the *crèche* could be made out of anything, come to think of it. "Why not have a game of hunting for things to create a manger?" he said. After all, there was hay in the barn, sheep's wool to make little sheep, wooden sticks to make the manger itself, and bits and pieces of fabric to make clothing.

"But what about the figures of Mary, Joseph, the shepherds and the Wise Men?" replied Jenny.

"Well," suggested their mother, "we could make them out of cardboard."

"I'll draw the faces," Jenny offered.

And so the two children began their Christmas away from home by thinking about what could be done in new and different ways rather than doing things the way they had always been done before. When the *crèche* was completed, their cousin was invited to look at the results. The girl had placed one of her tiny dolls in the manger and the boy had stationed some of his toy soldiers next to the Wise Men. The star was made out of a giant cookie with sugar sprinkles. There was a tree, *ein Weihnachtsbaum*, in the dining room next to the big clock. It was decorated with stringed berries, small cookies wrapped in tissue paper, and remnants of bright colored ribbons tied into bows. In spite of the war, there was even talk of some presents. Later, Cousin Sophie was caught staring at the *crèche* and even adding to it some of her own things, such as miniature porcelain dogs and glass birds from her very own collection.

The Christmas feast was indeed a reprieve from the routine of the farm. They had fried apple pancakes and herring in sour cream, although Cousin Sophie had substituted some other kind of fish for the herring. Next there were the Christmas *Stollen* and the plum cake, two magical gifts that reminded them of happier times in the lives of these displaced relatives. Cousin Sophie seemed to relax, and her eyes even sparkled at the merriment of the house. Throughout the district, the somber ways of living under the threat of war and privation were momentarily replaced by the gaiety and laughter of families who had gathered together for a holiday. However, these moments were few and far apart.

Somehow the hamlet near which the farm was located did not seem to feel the full atrocity of the war, at least not directly. Those who knew little of the machinations of the war and its leaders, humble souls like Cousin Sophie and the mother and her children, hid their overwhelming fear of becoming caught in the inevitable conflict of the two enemies by trying to remain on the margin of things. They were like tenacious reeds blown by the winds of a fascism running wild. They knew very little about ideologies and all the isms that made minds sway from rationality to irrationality, from compassion to brutality, from freedom to authoritarianism. What was an enemy to these people caught in the meshes of war? Who was the enemy? They certainly had no personal enemies. How could a person or an entire people become an enemy when they had never met a single one of them?

Only the fury of impassioned political speech or the mindless action of a powerful rabble-rouser could invent or create enemies overnight. Once the scapegoat was introduced into the minds of people, however, the enemy materialized. The worst kind of rabble-rouser is the kind that appears tolerant and merciful, the kind that shouts freedom but refuses to give it to others. This is the kind that flaunts superiority over inferiority, that hails utopias and perfection and never deviates from a sense of self-perceived duty and correctness. This is the rabble-rouser whose insecurity and constant sense of persecution makes him what he truly is— a being gnawed by the worm of human regression. These rabble-rousers are the real enemies. The infallibly righteous ones. The adversaries of those who accept their weaknesses and strive with their limitations, unafraid of baring them to others. These rabble-rousers are insidious, like rust and worms, and they throw the coldness of terror into the soul. Instinctively, simpler souls see them for what they are and seek to avoid any contact with them. Children and grown-ups who have retained the spirit of childhood know this, and it is usually reflected in their eyes, which are gauges of sincerity and fortitude. Unfortunately, many credulous souls are led to believe in the gilded promises of the rabble-rousers who would offer them bits and pieces of hope and progress, promises that remain vain and hollow. In the process, these promise-givers and passionate speechmakers become themselves the enemy of the people, since they offer only hatred and violence as a way out of problems and messes. They are the ones who twist things around and manage to play on the worst in people while diminishing the best in them.

While Gérard did not have enemies, he participated in what was being called "camps" or "sides." At school, he was on the right side of the class with some fifteen other students, while the rest were on the left side. *Deux bords*, the nun had told them. They competed in spelling bees, catechism answers, and other contests. At recess, they played on teams, and one side always came up the winner while the other side always came out the loser. Boys playing with marbles also had to face rivals. They would scoop out a hole in the soft mud and make a mound around the hole. Then they would push their marbles with the side of their index finger in one deliberate thrust so that the little glass ball would, if they were sharp enough in their aim, roll up the mound and down into the hole. Winner takes all! Or someone would devise some kind of wooden box with holes just big enough for a marble to pass through. To win, you'd have to stand on top of the box and skillfully drop your marbles through the holes. There were always winners and losers, more losers than winners. Very often, one boy's little cloth bag with purse strings would become empty while the ever increasing bag of some sharpshooter bulged with marbles.

Playing baseball, hockey, and other team sports always meant choosing sides, which ended up in the selection of the so-called worst player, the one who played like a sissy, the last one to be picked because they *had* to pick him. The teacher said so. And it was always done with disappointed grimaces. Always a question of winning or losing. After all, who didn't want to win? Winners and losers. How it hurt to be a loser. Winners always had the best things.

Smiles, medals, slaps on the back, holy images, stars affixed to their compositions, money, and even top choice when games were played. Nobody liked a loser. No one wanted to be one. Losers were like enemies, they were on the wrong side of things. Who wanted to lose a game? Who wanted to lose a war? America had never lost a war, so to be American was to be a winner. At everything. Gérard knew that.

Winning and losing was a boy's world. Girls didn't always understand that. Girls didn't like to play with boys because the boys always had to win. Sometimes mothers told the girls to let the boys win, so the girls retreated with their dolls and their skip-ropes to some other places where winning was not the only thing. Sometimes they played hopscotch with pieces of glass on squares and rectangles drawn with chalk on the sidewalk. They hated it when one of the boys stole their best piece of colored glass. Just to tease them. Just to be mean. What the girls especially hated was when some of the boys got bored with winning their own games and made sling-shot guns made out of wood and red rubber inner tubes. The rubber was cut into bands, stretched taut on the wooden barrel and released with a snap at the intended enemy, sometimes a girl, usually just to taunt her. Or the boys would play at cowboys and Indians, but none of the boys wanted to be Indians. So they would give candy to the ones who would play the bad guys just so they'd have Indians to shoot at. Even if they were just girls.

Children also saw grown-ups playing games and getting mad because they didn't win. The grown-ups got so angry when they lost that they started to use ugly words that were forbidden for children to use. Why? Because losers were dumb; they were laughed at. Losers, like the enemy, were below any sense of esteem. Some grown-ups told the boys not to play with so-and-so because they were losers.

Even the nuns didn't like losers. If you misspelled a word, if you had a wrong answer on a math problem, if you couldn't give a catechism response word for word, then you were a loser. They didn't say that, but you sure felt like it. And when it came time for report cards to be signed by parents, everyone knew you were a loser if your card was rumpled because you'd kept it in your pockets too long. Even when you had to bring home a slip from the Mother Superior telling your parents that you had not paid up your book account, everyone in the classroom knew you were a loser. Winners had money, lots of it. On Friday afternoons, while the children who were able to scramble the twelve cents needed to watch an Abbott and Costello movie or, better yet, a Dead End Kids movie in the school basement, the kids who were losers sat in a large classroom doing supervised schoolwork. All because they couldn't come up with the price of admission. Some parents were just too poor. They just couldn't find the twelve cents. The kids in the large classroom were losers, just like their parents.

Moreover, when word of the bad luck of neighbors who got laid off from the defense plants got around, everyone knew they had become losers. The girl who had to be sent away on account of a "she got in that way" affair, she was considered a loser, too. And how about the man who wore strange clothes and talked funny, not like everyone else? People laughed at him because they recognized that he was no winner. And the man who had drowned himself in the river on account of his losing his job? He was surely a loser. That loose woman who was whiplashed by so many tongues in the neighborhood? She certainly was no winner. And the neighborhood drunk?

Everyone knew who was a winner and who was a loser. Gérard certainly did. Sometimes, yes, it was difficult to spot the *real* winners and the *real* losers, but there were sure signs of being a winner. They drove the shiny cars. Their children wore nice, brand-new, store-bought clothes, even for playing out in the streets. Now that was being a winner. That's why mothers made the young ones get dressed up on Sundays. It was so they would be, at least for one day in the week, like those for whom God provided more than others. They'd be winners one day a week. Boys and girls thus grew up with the notion of winners and losers, and that's why during time of war the really big losers were the enemy, like the Germans. And all of their children were losers, too, because they were growing up to be enemies. They had to be. After all, enemies don't ever change skins; they never change at all. Their children and their children's children would forever perpetuate this ugly stain in their human makeup. Like the mark of Cain. People said so. At least, that's what outspoken politicians and people in the know proclaimed. It had to be that way. Why? Well, even the President of the United States and the Prime Minister of England said so. Of course, they used their own words, but they said, in effect, that all Germans were the enemies of righteous and upstanding people and the enemy had to be crushed at all cost. Wiped out once and for all. For many who took in all of these stirring words, the enemy meant everyone on the other side, the wrong side. Men, women, and children.*Everyone.*

CHAPTER THREE

Nineteen forty-three. Morgen's father is still in Italy mending the wounded. No word has been received from him since his last letter, months ago. Cousin Sophie has been training the children how to take care of the farm animals and the right way to pick herbs from the garden. Their mother has been teaching them to read and write; on certain afternoons, she has taken the road to the hilly side of the farm where she can sit and meditate on her own readings of art history. That is her only solace amid the fears and worries brought on by the war, however close or far it may seem to her. That and the protection of her family. Sometimes she encounters a young man with a limp who likes to hear of the faraway places where painters have left their mark. He has dark, dark hair with a deep blue streak that shines when the sun hits it just right, like the radiant slippery feathers of a black crow. His eyes are large, black, and deep as the night, and so intense is his stare that, it is said, it can penetrate one's soul. His complexion is that of a tawny peasant and his hands become wings fluttering in the wind. He hardly ever laughs or smiles. The mother can talk to him for hours about the Renaissance and the Neo-Classical and the Impressionist styles. Her favorite artists are Hans Holbein, Rembrandt, and Ingres. She likes Ingres, she tells the young man, because he controls his imagination. He draws superbly and his lines and color are most pleasing to the eye. To her, the *Odalisque* is a masterwork, incomparable in every way. Of course, she also likes the Impressionists as well as the Surrealists, but they are in a class by themselves. She doesn't like to pitch one painter against the other since, to her, that's barbarous antagonism. Every artist has his style and style is a hallmark of individual creativity.

Besides, art transcends national borders and likes and dislikes, she tells herself. She reads with horror how many works of art have already been destroyed by the disasters of war. Too many Monets and Pissarros were destroyed by fire and barbarian ignorance during the Franco-Prussian War, and how many Rembrandts and Titians are now being vandalized, stolen, or worse, destroyed by the war, she wonders. Of course, there was the Nazi art, the wholesome art of the Reich. While branding other artists as decadent, the Nazi regime and its artists helped to fill a void. Adolph Wissel and his "folk art," Hubert Lanzinger with his *Flag Bearer* created art that was used to convey ideas that were opposite of the Nazi true intent, or at least reality. The Nazi artists eschewed sophistication in subject and execution and came down to the level of the *Volk*, they said. All in the hope of inspiring the peasants while elevating the party's ideas. The mother does not like this kind of art. It has the look of propaganda and somehow masks the artistic freedom needed to really be creative. It just hits a bad nerve in her. How can they not know that art cannot exist without freedom, she asks herself, sitting up there on the hill. But in her heart she knows or at least feels that the Reich knows very well what it is doing by depriving art of freedom. It is manipulating those who give away their freedom too easily. These unwitting and hapless souls are swapping their freedom for some ideal that seems to be worthwhile, if not necessary at the time. Like bartering the air that you breathe for manufactured respirators. She will have none of it, she tells herself.

The young man with a limp, whose name is Helmut, likes to spend his idle time with the mother for he has few friends. So many young men are away fighting for the cause. He doesn't know if he would like to be with them or not, since he hasn't yet determined in his own mind what it is they are fighting for. He likes the fact that the Führer has brought the people, *das Volk*, into *die Nation*.

People, he says, can only take so much of humiliation and suffering in the soul. "My father tells me that being a people again is painfully but mightily right and no one should be able to take it away from us," he tells the mother. "Luther gave us our language and the Führer will give us our soul as a nation," he adds.

"But," asks the mother, "why must there always be force and violence with it, even with Luther?"

"Because sometimes we have to take what is ours. We must become masters of our destinies," Helmut insists.

"My husband is a pacifist at heart," the mother says, "and he must serve in the army taking care of mutilated young men. It's a work of mercy he is doing. I wonder how many French, British, and Americans would not even hesitate shooting him just because he is the enemy? Yet, he hasn't harmed anyone."

"Well, that's the way war works, dear lady," Helmut replies. "You have to choose sides. One cannot just be neutral, a one hundred percent pacifist."

"Why not?"

"Because human institutions do not operate that way. And, besides, human nature will not allow men to sit on the fence. One must defend oneself from the forces of evil, the forces of the enemy. From the forces of those who are out to get us, one way or another."

"But if everyone thinks that way, then everyone will come to bare their knuckles no matter how ridiculous it may seem at times."

"Fighting for what is right or for what we are is not always rational. It's a matter of justice."

"And," the mother asks, "just what is justice?"

"Oh, now that's a loaded question. I don't have the answer to that question, but I do have an answer."

"What is it?"

"Justice is."

"What do you mean by *justice is*?"

"Just what I said, it is. It doesn't need long explanations, especially not platonic philosophical expounding. What is due, that's all. If I own land and it's taken away from me, then it's just plain justice that

I fight to get it back. If someone hits me for nothing or takes some part of my honor away from me, then it's justice that I get even. If the government chooses to kill someone for killing another, I say that's justice. That's the law. Justice is. It is evident."

"But what about those who fall through the cracks of the law or whose destinies become tragic? How about the Jean Vaijeans or the Tristans of the world?"

"Oh, they're exceptions. There are always exceptions. We can't always stop for exceptions."

"Exceptions?"

"Yes, exceptions. Someone decides, one day, to write a story about a miserable man and his failures just to assuage his imagination. This author sells books. That doesn't mean that all is filled with injustice. The system works. Sure, it may not be right all the time, but it works."

"You haven't lived yet, my young friend," the mother says.

"What do you mean?"

"You haven't experienced the angst of deception and authoritarian power," she says. "Justice is often an ideal that emboldens men to fight wars and crush whatever comes between them and the enemy. I tremble at the notion that justice can be handed over to a system. Can a system dispense justice? Tell me, please tell me, Helmut, what is just? What is right? Can you? Can anyone?"

"Now you are using tactics to defend your mistaken idea of justice," he replies. "Justice is ... and when you're on the side of justice, you are on the right side."

The mother cuts him off and returned to her art history. "Let's continue our discussion on art," she insists, "or else, we are headed for a stalemate with no answers, just words."

"Yes, just like poets and novelists. Honest men use intelligence and action, not just words," he says with deliberate emphasis. Helmut then excuses himself and leaves

The mother returned to the farm and read a story to her two children. They were raised to love stories. They would often make up their own, but their very favorite was Grimm's tale of Hansel and Gretel. Everyone knows the horrible stepmother and the wicked witch, but what Morgen liked most was the adventure in the forest with the house built of bread and roofed with cakes and with windows of transparent sugar. Every Christmas, his mother made a gingerbread house and he was able to decorate it with her, using his every whim and every bit of imagination to come up with new and different ways of adding magic to the house. Cousin Sophie, on the other hand, much preferred the tale of the Cat and Mouse in Partnership to any other, for she claimed that in this story the nature of things is shown to be what it truly is and not the way someone might wistfully think it is. That natural inclinations don't change, and so people don't really change, no matter what. One must always be on guard, she said, for new leaders, new positions on things, and new ways of the big ones devouring the small ones come and go. She loved reciting this tale to the children and stressing the final lines, "And the poor little mouse, having "All-gone" on her tongue, out it came, and the cat leaped upon her and made an end of her. And that is the way of the world." And she would pretend to scrunch something in her mouth, all the while showing nests of tiny wrinkles around her eyes that were aglow with deep satisfaction. The children would jump up and run outdoors, filled not only with the wonder of the tale but with a kind of apprehension that any partnership could end up in such a way.

Meanwhile, in New England, every Saturday morning, Gérard would have his ears glued to the tall wooden radio with lighted dials in the living room listening to his favorite program, *Let's Pretend*. He liked the Pretenders, those Magic Makers who brought him to the land of make-believe, and later he would follow every word uttered by Uncle Bill, the host and narrator, even when he spoke of Cream of Wheat, the great American cereal. The boy would jump in with the sibyls into the magical mode of travel, be it a flock of crows, a steamboat, a train, or whatever.

His mind would be filled with the magical tales in the land of pretend while at the same time it also accumulated stories of the far away war so that even the war appeared to him, at times, to have a magical aura to it. It was happening in a land across the seas and one needed special travel to get there. There was talk of heroism, great battles, evil beings doing horrible things to others. In his *Pretend* tales there were witches, the Yellow Dwarf, and Bullovius, the giant of the beanstalk to contend with. Whether it was the enemy with the unmistakable black swastika or the enemy with a broom or a bludgeon, it was all the same to the young boy. The enemy was the enemy. Of course, in fairy tales, they were not called enemies but evil beings. Therefore, all enemies must be evil beings. It was as simple as that. Not just those who plotted and did evil things, but anyone or anything associated with them.

In one fell swoop, one giant black and white categorization, evil is evil, enemy is the enemy, because it was so. Besides, the enemy was really bad because one never prayed for the enemy. Not in Gérard's classroom. They prayed for good weather, for jobs, for crops, for sick people, for the dead, for soldiers far away, for victory in battle, for things to get better. But never for the enemy. Of course, Gérard also prayed silently for gold stars on his assignments, for winning more and more marbles, for good conduct grades so that his mother would not scold him, and especially for winning at baseball. He never, ever prayed for witches and giants, so why should he pray for the enemy? That would have been wasting prayers, wouldn't it? Besides, prayers were for real things. Enemies, although real in some way, were not entirely real to Gérard. He had never seen one. He imagined them much like he imagined witches, giants, dwarfs, mummies, and the bad guys he saw in the movies. Movies sure helped to make them come to life, though. What with their evil eyes, their humps, their scars, their limps, and their whips, they were really scary. But he had never met up with an enemy in his own neighborhood. He was glad that he lived in a safe neighborhood where none of that wicked stuff happened. And so, each Saturday was a kind of magical day for Gérard with *Let's Pretend* in the morning and the movie serials with the cowboys and Indians in the afternoon. Sunday was a day for church and getting dressed up with a visit to grandma's or to one of the many aunts and uncles. Sunday night was for homework that had not been done right after school on Friday as promised and revealed as undone to the bewildered mother who got after Gérard, as sleepy as he said he was, to sit down and do what he had to do without rushing. His mother would stand there muttering that this surely was not the way to win a gold star and Gérard would wonder if he might at least get the blue one, for he knew that the silver one was out.

From time to time, Morgen's mother met with Helmut. They talked not only about art, but also about theater and the censorship of books. That certain books, like those dealing with literature and philosophy, especially foreign literature, such books were burned in public squares. Technical books seemed to be all right, but books that spread unwanted ideas and could lead people away from concentrating on *die Nation* were not safe in the hands of people, it was said, especially works coming from those who could be termed radical. Such people could very well turn out to be bad for the nation. They would not be cohesive enough to help bind the nation together. They were the bad glue. They just did not fit. The mother remembered that, early on, books had been burned in front of Humboldt University in Berlin as well as in other university towns.

"Oh, how well I remember that," she said. "Can you imagine burning books, even art books? And worse of all, they were burned by professors and students alike. Burning their very own lifeblood! Censorship of classics, too. Do you remember when they removed Schiller's *Don Carlos* from the repertory simply because of that one line when Marquis Posa says to King Philip of Spain, 'Sire, grant us freedom of thought'? Remember? How barbarous we are becoming as a nation!"

Helmut found that a good part of this approach to censorship was fine, since he thought that some people went too far in absorbing into their lives strange ideas that stunt their own authentic identity, that of being a German first and foremost.

"Those kinds of ideas create problems and tend to twist people's minds," he said.

On the other hand, the mother replied, she considered all ideas to be liberating. "All nations need the sharing of thoughts and philosophies in order to grow as a nation. After all, great literature is universal in its ideas and characters. Human beings are human beings," she said. "And art is yet another form of ideas based on creativity that is universal. How can any form of art or literature be bad for people?"

Helmut replied that, surely, he was not for the burning of books. He would never go that far, but sometimes one needed to weed out things and especially be vigilant about the mores of society. There needed to be someone in charge of protecting the others from harmful products. "Take those who are the masters of degenerate art," he continued. "Chagall, Cézanne, Pechstein, Van Gogh, and Kokoschka."

"Now don't get me going," retorted the mother. "Besides, who is going to be that someone, that someone who decides for others? Who can truthfully say that he knows more than all the others? Who can say that he knows enough to be able to serve as grand judge over people's reading and discussions? Beware of people who claim they know best and set themselves up to be intellectually and morally superior," she told Helmut.

Helmut tried to interject his opinion, but the mother continued while his mouth remained half-open.

"I know this minister," she persisted, "in a suburb of Kassel who has set himself up to be in a supreme position over and above his flock. Everyone knows that he preaches the authority of the Bible and believes in the justification by faith alone. He is a proper Lutheran. However, everyone also knows that the good man has some severe ethical difficulties, what with his skimming the donations for the poor and harshly judging others for failures people know he himself has. He tells people not to do as he does, but as he says. That's fine, but after all, isn't he supposed to set an example for the very people he ministers to?" The mother paused and shook her head. "He is a very insecure man. He greases the palms of some, outlandishly praises others to extract favors from them, and steps over the poor and humble members of his flock not to have to associate with them. He is known for his repulsion toward the lame and the mentally ill. And he continually speaks of purity, purity of the kind, purity of those who must lead, purity both spiritual and physical as ordained by God. But do you know what is the worst thing about this man? He fervently believes that he is superior to others. Therefore, he justifies his actions by his own ego-twisted views on people and things. Now, there's a whitewashed sepulcher if I've ever seen one."

Helmut nervously switched topics. He spoke of the youth movement. "The *Jugend*," he said, "are in ferment. It's time to strike while the iron is hot. They need to be formed just so in order to have them become adults filled with integrity and with a sense of full belonging to *die Nation*. Our leader is right when he enlists the support of all of us to marshal the great energy of the growing generation so that the voice of *der Volk* can be heard loud and clear. Young people do not question, they obey. Thus, they learn to become true and unwavering to the *Vatersland*. Our future is in our *Jugend*'.

"That may be so," replied the mother, "but wouldn't it be worth our while as a nation to teach our young people how to question things so that they will learn to think for themselves?"

"No," retorted the young man," absolutely not. Do you want them to be misinformed and thoroughly misguided by believing that they can, by themselves, learn how to be true members of our society? You must teach young people that the high value and preeminent needs of society come before personal development and desires that often complicate things."

"Complicate things?" the mother asked, incredulous. 'How can the development of the human being as an entity complicate things?"

"It doesn't always serve the needs of *die Nation*, that's why."

"And just what are the needs of the nation?" asked the mother.

On the other side of the ocean, Gérard's mother was busy doing her laundry. She had gotten up very early that Monday morning, poured the hot water boiling in the huge copper boiler on the kerosene stove into the washing machine, and sorted out her dirty clothes. She then filled two large tubs, one she filled with hot water and bleach, in the other she mixed some Sawyer's bluing with the cold water. Once she had washed all of her clothes and rinsed them in the two tubs of water, the white fabrics in the bleach and all the pieces in the bluing, she got ready to hang her wash out by opening the shed window and stretching half of her body through the opening, nimbly and efficiently handling clothes pins, clothing, line, and pulley. Quite often in the winter, her fingers would go numb as she took the clothes off the clothesline, the various stiff shapes of shirts, underwear and socks. She always said that clothes off an outdoor clothesline smelled better.

Gérard's mother hardly ever stopped during the daylight hours. There was always so much to do, the washing on Mondays, the ironing on Tuesdays, the mending on Wednesdays, all the while thinking about and preparing the meals. Things were not always easy for a mother who had to spend so much of her time worrying about how the family was going to be able to make ends meet from week to week. It had been worse during the Depression when both of them, husband and wife, had lost their jobs at the shoe shop. There was no income, and they had lost the only home they were ever going to have. After that, it would be their lot in life to be renters, not owners.

However, now the war was on and the jobs were more plentiful. There was a glimmer of hope in their lives. She didn't care as much about long discussions on the meaning of the war as her husband did. He loved to talk and talk and talk about the war as if he were a bold general sitting in command of the latest events "over there." He would ramble on about how he would handle such and such a situation, always with a black and white certitude and moral righteousness. *No mercy for the enemy* was his byword. They all deserved to die; they all deserved to be wiped out. One clean swoop of the exterminating hand. He loved the military maneuvers of the Americans in command, for he did not think that the British or the French could handle the war, at least not to victory, not without the masterful lead of the Americans.

"We're far advanced in industry and much more ahead of the Europeans when it comes to warfare," he would emphatically state. "We saved them in '18 and we'll do it again in the 40s," he insisted.

The father, named Conrad after his godfather, thought that Roosevelt, with his work programs and the push toward greater participation in the fight for freedom around the world, was a mighty savior, especially for the common worker. The president was, for the father, a kind of god. He could do no wrong. Roosevelt knew by instinct who was the real enemy, and he would unwaveringly go after them. He had strength on his side, and strength was what counted in the father's eyes. Strength, according to the father, mixed with being right could provide enough force to destroy any enemy. The father had very little patience or tolerance for diplomacy; he called it being weak and namby-pamby.

"If we know we're right and we know they're wrong, then why not resolve the situation immediately without too much talk and dealings?" he asked. "After all, common sense tells you that right is right, and doesn't everyone understand that?"

So no bargaining, no long talks, no defending the enemy with smooth talk and wild ideas about stereotypes and generalizations. That was only talk anyway.

"Action! We need action and more action," he would emphasize with his fist banging the arm of the chair.

His wife, christened Albina but called simply Bina, would ignore him and his tirades about the war and the enemy "over there." "After all," she mused, "we have to take care of ourselves here in this country."

But, she was a bit perturbed about her husband's strong opinions on the war, since he had a tendency to have high blood pressure and this kind of talk did him no good. "Besides," she would mutter under her breath, "I don't like him expressing all those views about people he doesn't even know. Can all the people of a country be bad enough to be our enemy?" she wondered. "How about the children and the women who don't bear arms? The crippled, the mentally ill? When do people stop being our enemies?" she asked. "After the war? When we defeat them, do they remain our enemy? And the babies that come after the war? They grow up and become a generation of what? Enemies? The British were our enemies a very long time ago. when we were colonies. They were our enemies in Québec on the Plains of Abraham. Now they're our allies and friends. Will the Germans ever become our friends? Strange how the world goes, how one day you're an enemy and the next day you're not. Who decides?"

All of these thoughts ran through the mother's mind, but she cast them aside after a while, saying to herself that she wasn't educated enough, nor intelligent enough, to solve the world's problems. Probably not astute enough, either, to wrestle with the idea of enemy, she thought. "Anyway, people create their own problems and people need to fix them," she sighed with resignation.

Gérard was busy helping his father fix the family car. It was a black Buick with a boxy look, runners on each side, chrome headlights and grill, tan-gray plush upholstery, and even small shades on the windows that pulled up and down. The father loved cars, absolutely loved them, ever since his early teens. He loved to tinker with them, getting the oil and grease under his fingernails. Soiling his hands was his badge of honor. It was a man's work; a man needed to get his hands dirty. Only then did he really know that he was accomplishing something worthwhile.

"You can't talk about real work if you haven't gotten your hands dirty," he would tell his friend who was a second hand at the cotton mill. "You guys with a pencil stuck behind your ears are nothing but ass-kissers," he would taunt his friend. "You've switched sides, from workers to company men. All you think of is production and more production. We know we don't have much of an education. They hire guys like you to keep us in our places. They know you don't have an education, either, but you're worth a white-shirt job to them because they know, up there, they know we need the money, and people like you, one of our own, will always try to soften the blow, talk to us in our own language and make promises that will smooth things out. Damn company men! Only out to get us. You're one of them now."

He didn't say this in anger not even in jealousy, but he said it with a subtle yet nagging smile. The words bit hard. His friend, George—Tit-Blanc was his neighborhood name—never failed to answer him. He never followed up on his resolve not to mind him and his words about mill-workers.

"You are wrong," he said, "because you only see things with sides.

I'm not on any side but yours. You see, someone has to think for you workers. Planning must be done, orders carried out. Profits must be made to stay in business and that takes a lot of trouble-shooting and straightening out. Sometimes it gets dirty, not like the dirt under your nails, but dirty because people won't listen to reason. They're always ready to fight. They get mad and only see one side to things. Then they hate me for the job I have to do. But I'm on their side. I only want to protect them and their jobs."

"But who needs protection?" the father asked his friend. "We can take care of ourselves."

"You don't understand," George replied. "You don't know what goes on up there. They're watching you, they're watching me...."

The father cut him off. "And we're watching them."

Whenever Gérard heard his father and his father's friend exchange such words, he would quietly go behind the garage, following the path that led to the river, where he would almost inevitably meet one of his friends, who would be fishing. He would sit there silently watching his friend fishing while the waters gently lapped the smooth stones at the edge of the bank. There he knew he had a friend and he did not have to speak to him.

While Morgen was growing up far away from the cities, he managed to read and re-read every book he could put his hands on. He craved more books, especially books that would teach him about his country. When the mother asked Helmut to find her son books that would satisfy him, he told her that he had the right books for the boy. He would return in a couple of days with his booty. The mother did not question the many ways the young man had to get what he wanted. It was said that he had many connections. He certainly had no problems in getting books that dealt with ideas. They weren't always the ones that the mother wanted, but they were books to read and enjoy, not the technical ones that bored her to death.

Helmut soon returned with an armful of books. He had Goethe's *Faust*, Schiller's poetry, Büchner's *Dantons Tod*, Hauptmann's *Fuhrmann Henschel*, and even an early work by Thomas Mann. Mixed in was a volume of popular history for the boy. "Here," he said to

Morgen's mother "this one is for the lad. He should enjoy this since it deals with his country's great history from the *Nibelung* saga and the Nordics to Otto I the Great to end with Bismark."

"How about Rilke and Remarque?" she asked.

"They don't really count."

Morgen became an avid reader of historical works. Whatever Helmut brought him, whether it was the great sagas or the accounts of military ventures and conquests, he would sit down in a corner of the kitchen or on the feathery cool grass of the meadow to read his gifts from his mother's friend. She cautioned him about reading too much history and not enough of the creative imagination of the masters, but the boy persisted in what Helmut called *the proper education of the Jugend*. Morgen now accepted history as the solid demystification of the naïveté of fairy tales. For sure, he still liked those tales from his early childhood as entertainment, but he could no longer accept them as truth or reality. His mother wondered if this was just a phase he was going through or if it was the end of a child's dream world where the magic of myths and tales evaporates into the world of facts and brute reality, instead of slowly blending in with and eventually coloring the process of the age of reason in the growing up stages of a child. Had she not contributed to this sudden change in her son, she asked herself. She wanted her son to explore and expand as a person, not diminish and narrow. Cousin Sophie watched and waited, harboring mixed feelings of not knowing what was going on. She said to herself that all the boy was going through was the leap from childhood to good common sense as a developing adult.

One day, Morgen read about an incident that disturbed him very much. It haunted him for days. It was about a small village in the Lorraine region of France. The villagers did not want their domain ceded to Germany after the Franco-Prussian War. It was a humble village between Creutzwald and Forbach; one had a hard time finding it on a general map, but it was there on local maps. Tiny but strong, it was a village whose inhabitants had lived there from generation to generation and whose fierce and ineradicable strength and pride would not allow them to forsake their patrimonial allegiance. What the boy understood was that the villagers did not want to change sides, no matter what. They did not want to become Germans. They did not want to swear allegiance to another power just because someone had said they had to.

War had changed things. To the victor went the land conquered by might. Victory had made them the righteous owners and deciders. All of the other towns and their inhabitants did not see why this poor (some even dared say, insignificant) village insisted on being contrary to the others. Why would anyone want to cause so much trouble for an unimportant thing like changing sides? Because they wanted to remain who they were, not something that some lordly power wanted them to be. The villagers realized that the new authorities did not want them to move, but they did want them to change allegiance. They said no. They were going to remain who they were, even if it meant becoming neutral. Not choosing sides. Besides, who's to say if the whole thing would not change sides again? What if another war broke out and the victors became the losers? Then what? *No sides*, they said.

On an early spring day, the authorities came to speak to the villagers. There was no bargain to be made; it was a matter of swearing allegiance so that enemies could be contained. Potential enemies, at least. The villagers did not understand the authorities' insistence on enemies. They were not anyone's enemies. They simply wanted to remain who they were. They did not want to learn another language nor adopt other customs. It was explained to them that all they needed to do was to sign the paper that was presented to them, thereafter making them an integral part of the nation. How could a piece of paper change things? And why, they asked, was it so important to the authorities? They did not want to be one thing and officially proclaimed another. All they wanted was to be left alone.

Well, they were left alone for a while. Then, after the hassle had died down, representatives of the authorities—*enforcers*, as they called themselves—came to the villagers and took them by force to relocate them in some faraway locations. Some families were separated, while others escaped into the woods. Several people were clubbed into submission. The people couldn't take any of their possessions with them. Some fifty or sixty people were thus taken away, swept up by authorities who insisted that it was in keeping with *established law*. The villagers were so disoriented and disconsolate, for the commotion violently tore them apart, that they could not regroup. In the meantime, the authorities sent other enforcers under the cover of night to burn and sack the village. Everything was destroyed, not one stone upon stone remained. Fields were so devastated that they remained barren for many years and all traces of the village disappeared forever, its very name wiped out. Only the faint memory of those who forced themselves to remember it was left. Eventually some of the villagers came back, only to find nothing where once had stood their village. One man even tried to resurrect a tiny plot of land, but all of his efforts failed. No one came to his help and that year even the weather seemed to conspire against him. No rain for three months. Desolation and barrenness were all that remained of the former village between Creutzwald and Forbach, the village with no name because it insisted on being neutral.

Imagining the sad plight of the villagers, Morgen wept quietly. Later, his mother asked him why he wasn't reading anymore. He told her that he had not given up reading, but that he had stopped reading history books about Germany. He now wanted to resume his reading, but only when he could find the right book, one that would entertain him and not make him feel bad about himself and his fatherland. He didn't like books about taking sides.

Not too long after this incident, Helmut came hurrying to the mother with a gait that revealed his anxiety. He insisted on reclaiming, as soon as possible, the book that detailed the results of the Franco-Prussian War. He had given it to her without inspecting it and, besides, he told her, it was written by a half-Rom. It was not worth the time spent reading such jaundiced prose. Here, he insisted, was one book that should be burned. The mother returned it to him, heartened by the fact that such a small volume had opened up her child's mind and soul. In return, Helmut gave her a copy of *Mein Kampf*.

In New England, the weather had been wet and damp for days on end. People stayed indoors. For some, the weather affected their disposition, for they became less talkative. They became morose, even ill-tempered. It was time for storytelling and reading. Gérard's mother decided that the time had come to tell her children about her ancestors' past. They were the Acadians. *L'Acadie*. Land of the original French in North America, she said. They were the first ones, not the Québécois. La Rochelle was the area they originally came from. As for the mother, she came from a small town in the northernmost part of the province where Acadian blood thrived. Her own grandmother, who came from Bouctouche in New Brunswick, had told her the story time and time again. The story, the one *about le grand dérangement*, the expulsion of 1755 and a place called Grand-Pré.

The Acadians had been living peacefully as a group of farmers and landowners for over three hundred years. Many loved fishing, a trade they brought with them from the old provinces back in France. The new country they came to was named by Champlain L'Acadie, land of the fertile place. The rolling hills, the beckoning prairies, the dark rich soil, the lull of the ocean, all these fit their temperament very well. Of course, there were difficulties, too, like the rough winters, deaths at sea, wild animals that ate their crops, and the hard work required to make a living, but they were hardy people. They'd been hardened by adversity and the will to survive. They had even built dykes and planted grain on the reclaimed marshlands. Yes, they were a fiercely proud and independent people. They were solidly anchored on the shores of their land and rock-steady in their fields and farmlands. They felt they belonged in Acadia and would live and die in Acadia, prospering from generation to generation when their great-great-great-grandchildren could trace back their ancestry through name after name after name. All first names as repeated from one ear to the next from every stoop, every porch, every kitchen, each celebration by the village folk. Indeed, they belonged there; the land seemed to be made especially for them.

Although strongly independent, the Acadians could not stand aloof from the events of Queen Anne's War. In 1713, they were directly affected by the Treaty of Utrecht, which concluded the war and ceded Acadia to the British. There were two sides now, the British and the Acadian. When the British changed the name of the land from L'Acadie to Nova Scotia and decided to make it their own land, the Acadians didn't want to fight the other side, for the other side was more powerful. The Acadians didn't want to choose sides with the two archenemies in Europe: Great Britain and France. Could they count on the might of France? No. So they adopted a neutral political stance. The Acadians wanted to remain Acadians, no more, no less. As long as they were left alone and not pushed into rivalry and war, they lived at ease on their land. However, the presence of a large French-speaking unallied population in Nova Scotia was a cause of concern to the British colonial officials. The Acadians were considered a deterrent to British settlement of the colony. They had to go.

In 1720, Colonel Philipps, governor of the land, proclaimed that all Acadians must take an oath of allegiance without reservation or leave the country. The Acadians refused to do so because it would have provoked the Indians into thinking that the Acadians had become their enemy. Eventually, however, they were pressured so much that some took the oath, with a promise from the officials, however, that they, the Acadians, would not have to bear arms against anyone. Thus the Acadians became the French Neutrals, as designated by the British.

However, another war between the British and the French soon broke out. Nova Scotia was such in turmoil about taking sides that the British were forced to revise their attitude toward the Acadians. They would definitely have to take sides now, these Acadians, since they constituted a menace to the security of the land, which was British. The Acadians found themselves in a very awkward, if not dangerous, situation. More so now, since the British were really determined to fully colonize the land and were establishing over 2500 New Englanders in Halifax, the new capital of Nova Scotia. There was no way out. The Acadians had to sign. They sent delegates to the governor. Fear of Indian reprisals was lodged in the hearts of the brave Acadians, who wanted no part of the political maneuvering of their so-called conquerors. Delegate after delegate was put in jail.

In 1755, the Acadians protested against having their rifles taken away from them, rifles they needed to protect themselves and their crops. Wanting to put an end, once and for all, to these French Neutrals, Governor Lawrence issued deportation orders to Colonel John Winslow. All men and all adolescents, ten years or older, were summoned to appear at the church in Grand-Pré. The entire population of Acadians of the area sank into despair. Not knowing what was going to happen to them, they obeyed the order. They saw soldiers marching and boats approaching in the basin. The expulsion of the Acadians was soon in full swing. Men were separated from their families, kept imprisoned on ships, and allowed only occasional visits. Everything was in chaos. Mothers with young children tried to hold on to their belongings while at the same time overseeing the care of elderly parents.

Finally, in late October of the same year, a flotilla of fourteen ships set sail. The soul-shattering diaspora of the Acadians lasted for some eight years. The Acadians were sent here and there in the American colonies. Some escaped into the woods and headed for Québec. All of the colonies except Connecticut had not been warned about this mass movement of French-speaking people. Little or no hospitality was granted to these expelled people who had been forced to take sides and refused to do so. They were thrown like cattle into every foreign place where their own culture mattered for nothing. They were forced to travel as far south as the Carolinas and Georgia. Others from Cape Breton and Prince Edward Island were sent to England and France.

With time, some Acadians returned quietly to their land. They stayed far away from the officials and policy-makers. They tried to fit in to the vast land and its remote havens. Today, there are many pockets of Acadians in New Brunswick and Nova Scotia. They have regrouped, tenaciously holding on to the notion of their land, a notion anchored in their hearts that will not let go. Even though L'Acadie was wiped off the map over two hundred years ago, it still lives today in the very depths of the Acadian soul.

"It's called *belonging*," explained the mother.

The mother smiled as she looked at the faces of her children sitting there in quiet wonderment. The boy asked what the story meant for them.

"It means that we all come from somewhere," she told him. "We Americans, we all have roots. We mustn't forget that. Our history begins with a revolution, patriots fighting against compatriots. North America was conquered by both the French and the British. It was always a question of enemies."

"And the Spanish," added the boy. "They conquered America, too. Our teacher said so."

The mother replied in a mellow but firm voice, "So you see, in a way, we are all descendants of conquerors. The Indians were here first and we took it all away from them."

"The Indians?" Gérard asked.

"Yes."

"Boy, that's not the way the movies show it."

In the meantime, the father continued to read. He often reread his favorite stories. He especially liked John Steinbeck. Although the father had stopped going to school after the sixth grade because his parents wanted him to get a job, he had managed to nurture a habit of reading. Of course, he had his own ideas about things and remained unflinchingly steadfast about them, but, at least, he got to know that other ideas existed, even if he resisted many other ideas and accepted only a few.

"This writer knows how to deal with real people and events," the father would say. "He has a knack of delving into people's lives and making the truth come out."

The father had read *Tortilla Flat* and *Of Mice and Men*, but he preferred an earlier work of Steinbeck's, *In Dubious Battle*. Although the father had no sympathy for the reds and their way of thinking, he did empathize with the people, the apple-pickers and the vagrants, who had a very hard time shifting for themselves. They needed someone or something to get them organized against the big bosses. He especially liked it when action was taken on the spot to alleviate the condition of the itinerant workers. Sometimes it took violence to win, and the father liked that. He favored the actions and the words of Mac, the communist organizer and leader, although he did not approve of his philosophy. The father pointed to a section in the book where Mac answers London, the working leader, when he suggests that the guys "beat it." "Here's why," said Mac, "They can scare our guys, but we can throw a scare into them, too. We'll take one last shot at them. We'll hang on as long as we can. If they kill some of us the news'll get around even if the papers don't print it. Other guys'll get sore. And we've got an enemy. That barn was burned down by our own kind of men, but they've been reading the papers, see? We've got to get 'em over on our side as quick as we can."

The father could easily identify with the feelings behind Mac's strategy. He had himself participated in a strike at the local mill some years back. Sure, they'd lost the fight, but the fight itself had been worth it. That's what got the union in.

"You just can't work with one side," he explained. "Everything needs two sides and you just have to choose sides. Forget the gutless neutrals or the bleeding-heart pacifists. They don't fight for nothing and they don't deserve anything," said the father, as his wife looked at him and then at the children in utter bewilderment.

"Who stayed home while the others fought in the streets during the strike?" she asked him. "Not you. You were hiding in your garage."

And the husband, stricken by a sudden headache, retreated to the shed.

"This idea of sides and enemies," she murmured. "It's all a mess."

Gérard stood there, absorbing all of this in silence.

CHAPTER FOUR

The time had come for Morgen to go to school. It wasn't really a school, but occasional classes put together by retired educated townspeople for local children who wanted to learn more about such things as basic technology, the rudiments of botany, and the German language. Morgen had chosen botany because he had recently discovered a growing interest in the subject. His mother felt more comfortable with the townspeople now that she knew most of them. She had urged her son to go beyond the boundaries of the farm since she did not want him to become *ein wilder Einsiedler*, a wild hermit, and Morgen was getting tired of the old cousin hounding him about farm chores and of his sister, who increasingly wanted more of his time to play house.

It was at school that Morgen met Herr Kolossage (his name was a Germanization of the Hungarian name, Kolozsvar), who was a fourth-generation Magyar whose family had migrated to southwest Germany during the reign of William I of Prussia. Herr Kolossage was a teacher by profession, having received degrees from two of the most prestigious universities in Germany, the University of Heidelberg and the University at Frieburg. He had recently lost his position at the university where he had taught for fifteen years and been told that no explanation was necessary. He had no immediate family, only a distant cousin in the vicinity of the village of Rotkohl. Herr Kolossage's field was botany but he also nurtured a bold interest in anthropology. His hero was Friedrich Humboldt, naturalist and world traveler.

Morgen befriended the old teacher, and they got to know one another so well that Herr Kolossage began to confide in the boy about his love of anthropology. He recognized that the official position of the German government was against the teaching and propounding of ideas, especially those that conflicted with the official position of Himmier's *Schutzstaffel*, the black shirts, and the Gestapo. Cautiously but enthusiastically, the old professor began feeling out the boy about his family and their regard for the official policies of the country under the Führer. It seemed to him that Morgen had not been indoctrinated yet, that the boy had remained a child ready and frank like an open conduit for knowledge untainted by human exploitation.

The old master knew, or at least sensed, that something was wrong with the way violence was being used by Hitler and his men to build what they conceived as *die Nation*. Already he had heard rumbles about deportations and ethnic cleansing. Of course, he did not know the details, but his long years of trying to get at the truth of things in education as well as with his writings had fashioned him to believe in his gut feelings about things. He just knew that something was wrong, even though nobody was willing to talk about it. Silence and fear, yes, especially fear, molded people into robot-like creatures. Many did not want to know anything about anything except that life continued and that others were responsible for whatever was going on, right or wrong. If one did not talk about things, or even forced oneself not to think about them, they would go away. Besides, why should *das gutes Volk* be bothered with Jews and Gypsies, and, in whispered contempt, they would add, and those *homosexuell* degenerates? Purity of race and irrepressible indifference of noninvolvement seem to go hand in hand. Even if and especially if the major participants are uneducated peasants. According to Herr Kolossage, too much education fired up fanaticism in some people while not enough education bred not only lassitude but also contempt towards others who cannot quite measure up to ingrained standards of *Volk* values and behavior.

One afternoon after the other students had left for home, Herr Kolossage accompanied Morgen to the farm. He had received an invitation from the mother to have coffee with her. Helmut was able to provide the mother, once in a great while, with some black-market coffee. After the coffee and the big raisin cookies for the children, the master started to talk to the mother about his interest in anthropology. This led to some discussion about his travels and then the conversation wended its way like the flow of a river about present conditions in Germany. Topics like this were seldom broached outside of the strict confines of family or very close friends, since not only do walls have ears, but no one is to be trusted, it was felt, and intensely so. Absolutely no one. Trust was one thing the Führer's regime had totally demolished. It was even rumored that children could not trust their parents and parents could not trust their children. Nowadays, one had to be extremely careful about one's friends, even as old and trusted as they may once have been. Fear breeds all kinds of strange situations. One just had to choose sides and one very important side was one's own side, one's safety and survival.

Through months of personal contact with Morgen then with the mother, Herr Kolossage had won the confidence of both. They had now reached a point where hidden things could be shared, in strict confidence, of course. For sure, it had nothing to do with criminality or deep-down unpatriotic sentiments; it dealt with unanswered questions and a desire to know what was going on as well as a need to share one's feelings with another human being. And since the father had been away for quite some time, the mother needed that partaking.

The master talked about how he had gotten involved with anthropology and more specifically with the study of the Gypsies, the Rom. Botany was fine as a teaching and research discipline, he whispered, but he had wanted something more human, something more in touch with people's lives. Although the Gypsies were known for their rootlessness, their lack of history and homeland, and their reputation for being outsiders, which was synonymous with sorcery and crime, Herr Kolossage had found the study of Gypsies to be a fascinating one. His own ancestors had led a nomadic kind of existence prior to their emigration to Germany.

He had now discovered that not only were the Jews being deported to camps but so were the Gypsies and other social "undesirables," such as trade unionists, pacifists, homosexuals, and dissenting clergy. They had all become the enemies of the state. In the Nazi mind set, enemies of the *Volk*. He had heard that this had been going on for at least two or three years. This disturbed him enormously, and he just had to talk to someone about it. He related to the mother what he had heard about Lodzin Poland, where thousands of Gypsies had been gathered in a camp for extermination. It was underground news and one did not know just how to react to this kind of information. It was unbelievable! Devastating! Certainly he was on the side of Germany, his homeland, but he surely was not on the side of extermination even, God forbid, *genocide*. And besides, he felt so helpless not being able to do anything, not even talk about it.

He told the mother what he knew about the Gypsies, that they shared a tremendous feeling of not belonging, which they called *lungo drom* in Romani, their language. *Lungo drom* means "long road" and, basically, refers to the notion of no place to go and no turning back. The *lungo drom* constitutes a perpetual condemnation of the nomadic life. Gypsy songs are filled with nostalgia weighted with fatalism, for doom or fate is the heaviest burden of their heritage. They had become slaves under Prince Mad Dracul of Bulgaria in the 15th century. Herr Kolossage had read what historians had written about Gypsies. He had read that they "wished to become slaves, because this would raise them, if not to the level of human beings, at least to a par with good, domestic working animals."

"Can you imagine," he said to the mother, "not being able to feel like a human being? And besides, do you know that cargoes of Gypsies preceded African captives?"

"I can't picture the horror of such a situation," replied the mother.

"Beings like you and me not empowered to be human beings," exclaimed the master. "They are known everywhere as the enemy within," he continued. "It's no wonder that the Third Reich does not have any qualms whatsoever in persecuting them. To them, the Gypsies are 'lives unworthy of life,' as they put it. I overheard some people talking about Gypsies when I went to Poland last year to attend a conference about botanical drug experimentation. They repeated the very same phrase that I kept hearing about all antisocial or undesirable groups: *Lives unworthy of life*. Since then I have been keeping my ears open. Ever so surely, the truth is leaking out that our government is not only fighting a war with the enemy, but that part of the enemy is us, the people, at least some people, in our very own country."

"Now, now," said the mother, "that's very strong language, Herr Kolossage."

"But, don't you see, dear lady, that by rooting their idealism for a pure and unpolluted race and pursuing the unfair policy of the cleansing of *die Nation* for the greater good of the people, they have managed to create a *Volk* whose growing hatred of the undesirables grows like a beast unleashed? In the case of the Gypsies, they have become the target of contempt. Gypsies are considered to be the opposite of the *Volk*: unclean, darkskinned, devious, idle, and totally antisocial. The *Volk* now have an enemy, a total enemy."

"But how do you know that this is really happening?"

"I don't have any hard facts," the master replied, "no proof, but I know. When I put all my gleanings together, I arrive at one undeniable fact. There's something going on in our fatherland that will, some day, be considered to be an act of ultimate barbarianism. Watch my word."

"*Gott*," said the mother in a low voice. "I did not think that it was so bad."

Jenny called the mother to come into the house to help prepare the evening meal, and the mother and the master took leave of one another. As she watched Herr Kolossage disappear into the vast fields of tall grasses, the mother thought to herself what a nightmare this was and, then and there, she resolved to redouble her efforts to enlighten her children about all of this and give them, without putting them in peril, the necessary tools to become more educated about and sensitized to the fatherland's problem of dealing with all peoples. But, she asked herself, what could she really do about it? How would this war turn out? She didn't even know where she would go after the war. Home? Would there be a home left? And what about her husband? Could she count on anything anymore?

In the course of the evening, while Morgen was doing his homework for the botany classes, the mother kept a vigilant eye on her two children. Noticing her, Morgen stopped what he was doing and walked over to his mother. He softly asked her why she was forever glancing at him and his sister.

"Because I love you both," she replied, "and I don't want anything to happen to either one of you."

"What can happen to us?"

"One never knows."

"That's not an answer," the boy retorted.

"It is," the mother replied, "when your whole world has been blown apart."

Morgen and his mother continued talking and the subject changed to that of the Gypsies, since the master had already talked about the Rom to the boy.

"Mother," he said, "I've been looking at pictures of Rom, and all of them are dark-skinned with jet black hair and eyes and hands that flutter in the air. When I look at them, they almost make me scared."

"Why?"

"Because they do, that's why."

"My son, you should never be afraid of someone you don't even know. Do not fear the unknown and do not make enemies in your mind. Above all, you must trust the goodness of people whoever they are. Get to know them from the inside rather than from the outside."

"If everyone is good, then why are there evil persons?" asked the boy.

"That's hard to know." She replied. "I suppose because they have given up on themselves and on others. You see, evil lies in all of us and waits to come out. We must not let it overtake us, especially the evil of hate."

"But I don't hate anyone."

"No," she said, touching her son's cheek, "but hating, deepdown hatred, can happen to anybody. That's the enemy inside us all."

"Mother, is Helmut a Gypsy?"

After long thought, the mother answered the boy with a troubled look. "You know," she finally said, "I never even thought about that." She shook her head. "Don't you go making up things about people, especially about Helmut. We don't know, we really don't know.... Strange that I never thought of that before ... I simply thought that he might have some Italian blood in him."

Meanwhile, in New England, Gérard's mother was busy sewing a patch on her husband's overalls. She tried to make it as unnoticeable as possible; after all, she did not want people to think that they were poor, too poor to buy new clothes. As a matter of fact, with five children, she was forever trying to make ends meet. She found odd jobs here and there, but she could not afford to be away from home all day long, what with the care of the house and children, so she did low-paying jobs, like laundry. Her touch with the iron and especially with the starch was known to everyone who had seen her work. She starched collars and cuffs, aprons and furniture scarves to perfection, but her specialty was starching lacework. This was very difficult and painstaking, and she knew how to use just the right amount of starch so that the fluidity was perfect for lightness of body but stiff enough to reveal the intricacies of the lacework. Yes, she mused, the war had benefited some, but it had also bypassed others in extended gains. Besides, they never did have any luck at anything. War or peace.

There was a knock at the door. She stopped her work, set her iron upright, and went to the door. It was a salesman for Watkins products. She told him that she didn't need anything today and discouraged small talk by not inviting him inside the house. As she resumed her ironing, she thought of all the door-to- door salesmen she met during the course of one week, including the Fuller Brush man and the men who sold insurance. She did not mind those who sold encyclopedias and the children who sold chances, but she just hated it when the Gypsies came to her door selling paper flowers. She didn't like these women with their flowery skirts and gold baubles whose children looked so needy with their dark sad eyes. The Gypsies insisted and insisted until the mother, fearing that she might in some way offend them by refusing their flowers, usually wound up buying flowers just to get rid of the unwanted intruders. Besides, she had heard of their evil eye and wanted no part of it. Why didn't people like that stay in their own place, she wondered, and not bother those who did not go out and bother others? *Those Gypsies!* Why, she wondered, did they always seem underhanded and tricky? She didn't really know them, but she didn't like them. They were like bats in the night, filling one with fear and disgust. She didn't like them at her doorstep and didn't like them in the movies. There was always something of doom about them, she thought, something strange, if not evil.

That night, Gérard asked his father what KKK meant. He had heard it at school. The father began explaining that the Ku Klux Klan was a bigoted and violent anti-Catholic and anti-Negro organization. Members of the KKK were plentiful in the south. They burned crosses on people's lawns, lynched other people whom they said threatened the safety of an entire town. The KKK represented purity of national supremacy in some way that the father could not fully explain to his son.

Then the father started to reminisce about his own experience with the KKK on the bridge spanning the Saco River between the twin cities nineteen years ago. It was Labor Day and the KKK had organized a parade. The mayor of one city had given his permission to the Klan to march, but the other mayor had not. In fact, he was categorically opposed to the march, which he denounced as lawless and violent. Many of the Irish met the Klan with rocks in their hands, while some of the French-speaking people, it was said, carried knives in their pockets to use against the Klan. And so the Klan stopped their march right there in the middle of the bridge. Fortunately, no one was hurt. Gérard then asked his father if he had a knife in his pocket when he met the KKK. The father first said that he did not remember. Then he said in a haltering voice, "No, I guess not. We didn't have any sharp knives in the home. No hunting knives."

"But you were there, weren't you?" asked the boy.

Gérard's young life was already intertwined with the history of his country. Want to or not, he was learning at school that as part of his belonging he had inherited a vast background of historical happenings and choosing sides.

One such major happening was the Civil War that had split the country. At issue were the rights of the states and the rights of the nation and its individuals. After all, every citizen had been guaranteed "life, liberty, and the pursuit of happiness." But it seemed that these rights were not for everyone, especially not for the poor, whether black or white. So the young nation fought over the right of people to own slaves. After all, some said, slavery benefited everyone, especially the blacks, since they had been rescued from savagery. Yes, they said, saved from the deep, dark bowels of African pagan ignorance. Furthermore, masters had a right to their own property and slaves were constitutionally protected property. The United States Supreme Court held in 1857 that a slave taken to a free state was still property; the judges held that slaves were not to be considered persons but property. Owners had a constitutional right to reclaim their property. That was the law. The law was on the right side of things since law meant justice and justice meant the right thing was being done. Everyone knew that. Property was property, no matter what. As a member of these United States of America, a landowner had specific rights. Slave owners had specific rights. It followed that ownership and right to possession went hand in hand. Established law just could not allow the right to property to be abrogated just because a certain property happened to be a slave, property not considered human; after all, they were niggers, and niggers were below soul-endowed human beings. Besides, they were not only inferior but even bad at everything they did. Every highly civilized society knew that. Didn't the French have an expression about speaking "bad" French when they said *parler petit-nègre?*

Although Gérard didn't understand everything he read about the Civil War, every nuance and inference, he understood enough to make him feel a bit queasy about what he was reading. It made him feel that somewhere, somehow, black people had become enemies. But whose enemy? They certainly had never openly chosen sides. Their ancestors had been forced to live under the domination of those who were considered to be in the right, and so each succeeding generation suffered from the allocation of rights to the few who controlled the many.

What Gérard was learning and learning fast was that there were sides to everything. Besides, if the young Gérard had known everything that existed in history books about slavery, the Civil War, and the Industrial Revolution, his mind would have been overwhelmed. But, of course, he was too young to even imagine the extent of the complexity of the situation. He would have to grow up; maybe then he would understand. What he would eventually find out about the historical facts was that slavery and Negro labor were considered to be absolutely necessary to Southern prosperity. Society as a whole benefited, they said, because there was no real unrest or real poverty. Wasn't the South supplying the world with an essential commodity? Cotton. The North had its cotton mills and the South its cotton gin. Everybody benefited. Eventually, Gérard would learn that New Englanders had worked for industrialists who benefited from slave labor. Besides, his very own people, those who had come from French-speaking Canada and had been working in the mills for generations, they also had been considered to be almost slaves when a government consultant had branded them the "Chinese of the East." Docile and stupid, he'd said. And so the struggle went on. Yes, there were sides to everything; it was inevitable that all relationships, all situations, all geographic entities would fall into sides. Would the human factor of interrelationships ever develop into one, holistic, equal, and allied body? A better question yet—*could it?*

And then there was the question of the Japanese-Americans, those who were sent into exile because they were considered an extension of the enemy over there. Although President Roosevelt had called the day Japan bombed Pearl Harbor "a date which will live in infamy," the infamy had another side to it: the imprisonment of thousands of Japanese-Americans, many of whom had been born in the United States, just like the young Gérard. But of course, Gérard had white skin and "regular" eyes, not slanted ones. Yellow skin and slanted eyes made one an enemy practically overnight.

The U.S. government emptied orphanages and foster homes of every child with even the slightest amount of Japanese blood. Men, women, and children, even babies, were considered enemies of the true American people. Yes, babies were rounded up like evil beings and banished to a place called Manzanar, a desolate windswept stretch of land in the foothills of the Sierras in northern California. Defenseless, but somehow a threat to the American way of life, they were taken away by the military police. They were, after all, *the enemy.*

Gérard would later learn, much later, when things finally came out, that orphan children, truly American children, had been abandoned twice, once by their family and once by their country. Just because they happened to have had Japanese parents. Even only one Japanese parent. One drop of Japanese blood was enough to make these children enemies. Even those in foster homes were disposed of over the objections of their foster parents. All things were done systematically. Social agencies identified them. The Western Defense Command and the Fourth Army were there to enforce their internment. Considered aliens, these Japanese-Americans were nevertheless as American as Roosevelt. But they were on the "wrong side." These classified enemies of America put behind barbed wire were confused. Who had chosen their lot for them? They were Americans, they said, as American as the Italians, the French, the Poles, the Irish, the Spanish, and the rest of them who had come to settle in the United States. Well, yes, they looked like the enemy. That was enough for many Americans. After all, national security was at stake here. Some sacrifices had to be made, even if it meant imprisoning some and clandestinely pursuing others, like the German-Americans and even the Italian-Americans. In all of this, fear was the real culprit, the real enemy, but few Americans noticed and too few cared. "We have nothing to fear but fear itself," came out of the smooth mouth of the nation's fearless leader. Yeah, like fear to be seen in the eyes of children and babies considered to be enemies.

You know what was really crazy about this whole incident, Gérard would later tell himself, is the fact that some of these very same interned Japanese-Americans were drafted into the army. Some even volunteered. They all served patriotically and with honor. That's what is so irrational in this fear of the enemy.

When you fingerprint a six-year-old and tell him that his heritage is bad and that he had better be on his best American behavior at all times, or else, that really stunts his self-confidence. It was done repeatedly to the children who were being released from the camps after the war. Stamped with the mark of Cain, the evil one, the enemy. When will it ever end, Gérard asked himself when he discovered this tragic response to fear on the part of his country in the forties. He would have to wait many years before he could come to grips with such a thorny problem.

Right now, Gérard was too young and too busy to be preoccupied with history and ideas beyond his capacity to grasp their full meaning and immediacy. He needed to grow up and enter the adult world where all of these things would eventually be unscrambled. Or would they? All he knew right now was that he wanted desperately to be on the right side. He wanted to be with winners. He wanted to join the Red Sox some day. They were real winners. Pennants and even the World Series perhaps. Someday, he thought. In the meantime, he needed to finish his chores or else his mother would tell him, in no unclear way, which side he stood on.

CHAPTER FIVE

NINETEEN FORTY-FOUR

H-I-M-M-L-E-R, Heinrich

Born: October 7, 1900
Place: Munich, Deutschland
Father: schoolmaster
Education: [non-vital information]
Rank: Minister of the Interior;
Commander-in-chief, Home Forces
Appointments: by the ReichsFuehrer
Race: Aryan white
Religion: [non-vital information]
Note: considered to be the most powerful man in
Deutschland after the Führer; a most capable and
industrious man. An organizer without peer.
(Indispensable.)

Heinrich Himmler, the organizer, technocrat, follow-up man, administrator who executes orders to perfection, and profound believer in authority for authority's sake, had applied the dictates of slavish conformity to what he considered to be the law of excellence in administration. He had demanded systematic cataloguing. He had even made a catalogue card on himself. How could he not? After all, he was the most powerful one among many in the Nazi regime. (But he had not dared to make a card on the Führer, even though he had his medical record.) Eichmann had a card, Göring had one, Hess had one, even that stupid Goebbels had one. So why not have a card on the master designer and executer, he had told himself. After all, he was in charge of all classification and the pursuit of necessary information on people. Deutschland demanded it. For the sake of purity, stability, and progress. Everyone must fit in. No deviance. No misfits. No marginal behavior. No recalcitrants. No physical, moral, or intellectual hindrances. None. Cartesian and Pascalian truths gone haywire. *Tabula rasa. I purge therefore I am. L 'instinct utopique a ses raisons que la raison ne connaît pas.*

H I M M L E R. He who was the perfect misfit of insecurity and intellectual mediocrity, his behavior was by every means deviant. Notwithstanding, a deviant penchant does not tolerate deviance very well. HIMMLER, Heinrich: Master and Protector of the Master Race. The consummate technocrat who meticulously and ceremoniously piddled his way to the top.

In Germany, things were not going well; in New England, things were going on as usual. The year 1943 had been a catastrophic year for the Deutschland with the disastrous event in Stalingrad, the capitulation of the German army to the Sixth Division, and the loss of Tunisia, the last stronghold in Africa. It was the same year that Himmler addressed the SS leaders at Posen, where he ranted about those who would dare stain and dishonor the laws and principles of Germany and its military, those like the gutless *Homosexuellen* and the mealy *Pazifisten.* The SS were the guardians of the trust that the *Volk* had held on to for thousands of years. Like the virile depth of the virginal forests, he proclaimed, the *Volk* are deeply rooted. The *Volk* are like a huge tree extracting its lifeblood and purity from the soil. The *Volk* are ever striving for the sun, for they are *Lichtmenschen,* people of the light. As guardians of the *Volk,* the order of the SS is akin to a medieval chivalric order, defending, safeguarding, and exemplifying the noble ideals of the very soul of the *Vaterland.*

Himmler had modeled his elite group after the knights of yore. Therefore, the subhumans, the demons, the rootless and the shallow ones all had to be weeded out. Cut down by the invincible sword of the dragon slayer. After all, the subhumans were not the chosen ones. The chosen ones had roots, deep roots in the land. And the land needed to be protected from all kinds of filth. The roots needed purity, purity of soil and growth. Himmler raved for hours to his captive audience. They were the chosen ones. Chosen by the authority of Aryan destiny. They were the protectors of *die Nation*. As the leader of this virile, manly force, Himmler dared to envision a new millennium, one that would proclaim the transcendental essence of the German people. The Tree People. He felt he himself was at the very summit of the tree, his feet deeply implanted in the soil of Deutschland. That speech was one of the truly glorious moments of his administrative life. Leaders, he told himself, need glory in order to support the strain of responsibility.

But now Himmler was scared; he was alone, by himself. Things were not going the way he had planned. Why would they not go according to plan and schedule? After all he had control of everyone between twelve and seventy. He had just been appointed Commander-in-Chief of the Home Forces, the most powerful man after the Führer. *He was in control.* He sat down with his little dog, Wölffchen, and remembered the time he had saved the Führer's life and had been rewarded for it. Now the Führer seemed to be losing control, even with the *Jugend*, and someone had to take charge. "Leave it to me, my little Wölffchen," he said. "I will manage things. I will set order to things. I've always done it before and I will do it again." Himmler liked to talk to his little dog, Wölffchen, because the little dog always listened to him with wide-eyed enthusiasm.

To show that he was indeed in charge, he sat down at his desk and listened to "the voice out of darkness," as he called it. He liked the darkness because the dark shielded his eyes from the harshness of the sun, the blaring light of day. How he hated the light! He liked to watch his mind work in utter darkened quietness. He marveled at all the master plans he could come up with all on his own and then implement by giving orders to those he controlled. He pulled out a long piece of paper from the middle desk drawer, laid it on the desk, and with a sweeping motion of his right hand affixed his signature at the bottom. He had just signed an order placing all Gypsies, "those rootless Roms," as he called them, under arrest. They were to be sent for experimentation, to their deaths. Experimentation on the Gypsies would indeed serve the war effort, he told himself. He then quietly shut off the light and went to bed without a single worry of what tomorrow might bring. Like a contented cat having eaten its prey, he sought the comfort of sleep.

Dawn was breaking when the hamlet on the outskirts of Bernau where Morgen was living heard the news that Hitler had been assassinated. There was turmoil, there was confusion, there was utter disbelief. There was even joy on the part of some. Finally, they said, this madness would soon end. But was it all the Führer's fault, some asked. He was the authority who guided them, but now things seemed to be going haywire.

At first, everyone had been convinced that they were on the right path with Hitler. The German people were back on track, they said. They had found their destiny, that of a strong people beholden to no one and under no one's power but their own. But now ... things seemed not to mesh together. The people had been deprived of necessities, especially food, for the good of the war effort. Although they had steadfastly cooperated with the high command, they had become a sullen people. They obeyed, although at times they did so a bit begrudgingly, but always in silence. Now something had cracked like a giant bell that had been celebrating all along the victories of the army, the navy and the *Luftwaffe*, the best organized and the most powerful army in all of military history. The giant bell was cracking. The glorious peals were now death knells. Ominous and gloomy. Where was the voice that proclaimed the right path? Where was the voice that told them how they could gather strength, as weak as they were, and outlast the protracted war effort? After all, there comes a time when the mind can no longer take it, a time when the body has already given up. But they had to believe in something, someone. The Führer just could not die!

Well, the Führer was not dead. It was just rumors. It had been, they said, a British ploy to further weaken *die Nation*. It was reported that the British had forged German stamps with the face of Heinrich Himmler to encourage rumors that the SS chief had planned a coup against Hitler and had ordered the stamps to be issued afterwards. Enemy agents inside Germany had used the six-*pfennig* stamps to send letters to neutral European countries. An initial mailing to Sweden failed due to what some people called the unobservant nature of the Swedes, but eventually the stamps produced the desired result. A Swiss newspaper reported speculation about the coup. Now it was reported that the mailings had just been expanded to Spain, Portugal, and Morocco. Just yesterday, people said, the authorities at the *Reichstag* had issued a statement admitting the stamps had been published in error. What were people to think of all of this? It appeared that even Himmler could not control the flow of things. Even Himmler could not order the credibility of what was going on.

Meanwhile, in Lausanne, Switzerland, the 19:14 train from Milan, Italy, arrived on time. On board was a passenger who carried a bundle in his right hand, wore his hat pulled over his eyes, and walked with a hurried gait to the exit on to the platform. He looked gaunt and tired. He wore the scragginess of an unshaven face like a lost man in pursuit of some safe harbor; his eyes were reddened by the lack of sleep but intense in their gaze. He was alone, moving with the swiftness of a desperate soul, and no one seemed to notice him as he walked outside the train station. He automatically put his right hand to his breast pocket and checked inside to see if his passport was still there. Of course he knew it was there, but he just wanted to be reassured by the presence of a flat little booklet that verified his identity if not his existence. It had become his obsession, this passport, since it was what liberated him from belonging in this turmoil called war. But he asked himself, to what did he belong? Certainly not to his passport, nor the country which had issued it, Italia. He had lost his original passport; it had been confiscated by the commandant of his section. He had managed to buy another one, this one with a foreign identity, because he had to get away from the torture of being mixed in with the victims of the war. He silently called himself a pacifist, a term not well-received by the German high command, especially the Gestapo. But that's what he believed in. It was seared in his heart and had long protected him from the ravages of guilt and shame.

He had not voluntarily joined this massacre; he had been forced to practice his skill as a physician in the midst of carnage. He wondered if he was a coward. His German blood stirred every time someone mentioned pacifism and cowardice in one breath. All he knew was that he had chosen peace in his heart over violence as a way out of the shame after the armistice ending the first war, when the French had shoved German noses into the muck and mire of retribution, shame, and dire poverty. "One does not recover honor by inflicting pain and destroying nations," he had told himself. Still, as a German, he wondered when this turmoil of retribution would end. If ever. Right now, following the defeat in Stalingrad, it did not look too good for the German army. After the war—he knew that ultimately it would end—after the war, what would the Russians do to the Germans? And wouldn't the French and the English pursue their revenge on the German people? When would the Western world learn that peace is not gotten by retribution? "It's earned," he whispered to himself, "one deliberate fragment at a time."

The physician was still in a daze when someone asked him for his passport. He had almost caught himself blubbering in German when he realized that the uniformed officer was staring at him. "*Italiano?*"

"*Si.*" He then explained that he was Italian on his father's side. Neapolitano. His mother was of German origin, he informed the guard, and that accounted for the blond hair, but the eyes were Italian, brown like the pope's, he insisted.

"Yes," said the officer, "Pacelli. Salvatore Pacelli, born in Capua. *Come lei piache ii volcano in Capua?*" "Oh, Signor," replied the bearer of the passport stamped Pacelli, "but there is no volcano in Capua."

The officer signaled him to pass on.

The man did not know where to go. He looked around and wondered what he would do next. He checked his pockets, he had a few lire, a couple of German notes, and some Swiss francs. He knew that he could not afford a decent hotel. He turned left and kept walking briskly into the shadows of buildings. He kept away from strong lights, as if he had become a lone wolf or a vampire. He told himself that if he had become an animal, afraid and hungry, it was because the war and the system had forced him to be so. He had not chosen to be what he had become. An animal now, burrowing his way out of the confusion that had turned his world upside down. One can probably begin to understand war waged at the enemy, but war also had another side to it. It involved your own people, your neighbors, your relatives, your friends.

How can one justify repairing one's honor with the torments and killing of one's own, he muttered to himself. No honor is worth the spilling of blood. But who am I to renege on human history and so-called virile moral valor? But, he told himself, as long as there is one pacifist alive and breathing, there is a small hope for humanity. After all the wars, the skirmishes, the violence of fist fights, and the grudges held that explode into virulent hatred, one would think that we humans would have finally learned something, that violence is not the way out but the way into the mire of shame. Words and thoughts, he muttered, are cheap. I needed to do something. To get out of this mire of smoke and mirrors. I thought I was helping out those brave soldiers by cutting them up and repairing their bodies, but I was fooling myself. I was simply protracting the war effort. My place is with my family, where I can really help those who are dear to me and my country. Probably, this *Vaterland* will eventually learn what I and others like me have to teach it by example. But where will I go now? He kept on plodding until he arrived at a small hotel squeezed between two large buildings. With its two small windows, circles of reddish light attracting neither visitors nor natives, only the drifters who seek shelter for the night, it looked like a tall, spindly creature peering out on the alley. It was the Hôtel Petit Bonheur.

The man looked around, wondering if he should enter a place that sent shivers up his spine. But he had no other choice. It was either this place or the street. He gently opened the door and saw a woman fixing her hair behind the counter. Her yellowish-brown hair had no luster, her makeup was thick, and her eyes seemed friendly in a taunting way.

«*Quest-ce que vous désirez, Monsieur?*» she asked him in a sweet but rasping voice.

«*Une chambre,*» said the man.

«*Pour la nuit avec une heureuse présence?*» she asked him with a quick wink of the eye.

He shook his head, no.

«*Ça alors,*» she said. «*C'est neuf francs,*» and she went on to inform him about the rules of the house.

He suddenly understood that he was in some kind of brothel that allowed visitors to spend *la nuit incomplète*, as she put it. He climbed up the stairs, found the number on the door, and went inside the room. Without turning on the lights, he put his small bundle down and threw himself on the bed. His head went swimming in the dark. He started to relive his wartime experiences in Italy with the wounded and the battle fatigued corps of so-called healers and practitioners such as he. How could he help heal in a place where extended butchering was all that one could do? The poor bodies had been butchered out there. Now they expected us to put them back together so that they could either be sent back or placed in some kind of hospital where these sad boys would linger for months, if not years. Doctoring becomes madness when lives are being butchered over and over again. 'I'm a doctor," he said aloud to himself, "not a butcher, for God's sake!" He slowly fell asleep. He woke up suddenly to find himself in a dark room with no toilet. Of course, he knew better. He opened the door, walked down the hallway and found the communal bathroom. As he was walking back to his room, he crossed paths with another man who merely mumbled a few words in French to him without making eye contact. He did not respond.

Early next morning, he went to wash his hands and his face before leaving the hotel. He checked his bundle and his breast pocket.

His passport was missing! Someone had pilfered it during the night, he knew it. Passports were in high demand these days. They could bring in a lot of money. He had spent a great deal just to get this one. Gone was his abbreviated feeling of security. What would he do now? Without a passport he would have to keep on playing the drifter, for the man without papers might very well become the hunted. He would certainly talk to the woman downstairs about it. He had to get the passport back.

She told him no, she had not seen it and that after all, this hotel was a safe one, not always the most reputable one, but people here did not go around stealing things from others, especially not passports. Then he thought of the man in the dark hallway. He rushed upstairs and went from door to door trying to find out if the man he had seen in the night shadows was still there. He met no one. In despair, he went downstairs. As he walked outside, suddenly he felt a hand on his left shoulder. He turned around to face a man with a hat and a checkered overcoat with a small cape over the shoulders.

"I don't want to scare you," the man said, "but I know you lost your passport and I wanted to reassure you that it wasn't I who took it."

"How did you know that?"

"I overheard your conversation with the woman at the desk. It was me you saw last night in the shadows of the hallway. I think we were the only ones who spent the night."

"I don't know what to do anymore."

"Can't you go back to the country of origin?"

"I can't."

Somehow the man seemed to discover a certain amount of trust inside himself, just enough trust to confide in this person who appeared to be genuinely human and compassionate. "I know I'm naïve," he said to the stranger in the checkered overcoat, 'and I may live to regret this, but right now I need someone in which to confide. I cant live like this any longer, from hideaway to train station to nowhere. I should learn to be more careful about such things, but if the day comes when no one can trust another human being, then it's time for me to disappear entirely." The physician sighed. "You look like a gentle person, a kind person who would do no harm to another like himself. I don't think you're with the Gestapo, nor an enemy nor a thief, and so we are brothers in passing who have spent the night in a dump like this in order to move on to the next journey. Am I not right?"

"Listen," the stranger said, looking up and down the street, "before you disclose anything to me, please make sure that you want to do this."

"What choice do I have?"

"Well, you could walk away."

"And do what without a passport? Run and hide alone?"

The stranger sighed and shook his head. "What can I do to help you?"

"At least listen to me," the physician said, "and provide the company I have so longed for. You see, I escaped from the war hospital in Naples. I couldn't take it anymore. I ran away. I'm a doctor, and a pacifist at that. It was either escape or the concentration camp. I wanted to protect my family from disgrace and starvation, so I went to war without revealing my convictions and my repugnance for atrocity. I was German. I was a man, a doctor, a father. I was part of that promise of a better life after we had overcome and crushed the consequences of the reparation act after the first war. I was willing to sacrifice my ideals and convictions for the safety of my family. Its not what we would call strong moral convictions, is it?"

"I don't know what to tell you," said the other man. "All I know is that ideals and convictions are only worth their salt in times of decision-making. Even then, they sometimes get in the way of reality. We need to sort out our priorities. If you're going to hurt the ones you love in the process of sticking to your convictions, then what have you gained? It's nice to be noble and act like a knight, to be willing to cut down the dragon in the fight for right and wrong, but what is more important, ideals or the people who trust you and love you? Don't get me wrong," he said. "Everyone needs ideals, but not at the expense of others. Listen, I have lost Sons to the war, one who even committed suicide in order not to be part of the killing. I know what a true pacifist is. I know the price one has to pay for a peaceful heart. Not only did I lose sons. but I also lost the love of a daughter who could not tolerate having a father who is what she calls *not a true man*. I lost family, home, and even now, country."

"Where are you from?" the physician asked.

"From Austria."

"I'm from Kassel."

"Two Germans in a dark alley in Switzerland."

Both men started to laugh. "Let's get out of here," said the Austrian, patting his checkered overcoat, "before we get into trouble."

They reached a small café on the outskirts of town that was not frequented by many people. They ordered coffee but the *garcon* told them that they only had some kind of substitute coffee and diluted hot chocolate. They chose the *café orge*, as it was called, and sipped the steamy drink even as they squinted their eyes in distaste.

"I'm a vestigial Jew, you might say," said the Austrian in a low whisper. "They, the Gestapo I suppose, found a bit of Jewish blood in my ancestry dating back five generations. Even that so-called distant relative is cause for debate, since she may or may not have married into the family. All they know about her is that she had a name that sounded like or looked like a Jewish name and was associated with our family line." He shook his head. "As far as I know, she might have been a maid who had a questionable relationship with one of my relatives. The fact is, this documented or undocumented relationship was enough to raise the question about the authenticity of my Aryan bloodline, as the officials put it. In any case, it did not matter. Nothing mattered when I was classified by Himmler. They took my passport and handed it back to me with the red J stamped on it. *Jüdisch no longer Arisch*."

"Didn't you appeal?"

"Appeal to whom? To the perpetrators of this scheme? I had no other choice but to run away as soon as I could. I guess being Jewish, if only by inference or doubt, I should be your enemy, too, an enemy of the German people."

"But you are my brother by citizenship and heritage."

"Yes, I know, but God forgive those who measure the quality of a man by his ancestry and his blood."

The Austrian paused for a moment and then added, "Did you know that the red J was the concoction of a Swiss physician, Dr. Rothmund, who was head of the Swiss Immigration police in 1938? The Nazis adopted it enthusiastically. What better idea than by official identity to segregate the wheat from the chaff."

"Separating identities never entered my mind," the physician said. "We are, after all, one people. If we start to fragment our people we will lose the nation that we are."

"Oh, but my dear friend," said the Austrian, putting down his empty cup, "they are implementing the very death of the nation that once was by sending thousands of Jews, pacifists, Gypsies and others to hidden camps. Trainloads of them. I don't really think the Gestapo is sending these people away just to be *contained*."

"But how can that be? We are not a nation of slave-makers, nor are we a people of executioners."

"No," the Austrian said, "but there are some elements disguised as ideals and supremacy that eat away at our very flesh and bones. If you strip away the skin of Nazism you will find the worm."

"What do you mean?"

"The worm that is Himmier. And his knightly men, as he calls them. He is now filled with power up to his neck, and he relishes it. He's been made the Commander-in-Chief of the Home Forces. What is a fiendish little man like that doing as Commander-in-Chief? Why, he's near illiterate and assuredly devoid of any sense of creative esthetics. He's all organization and cold-blooded efficiency. As a puffed-up functionary, he functions; he doesn't live. That's what becomes of someone who stops at nothing, not even decency. Mark my word, my friend, some day soon, even our Führer will dispossess him. He's not only dangerous, he's evil. I say a man devoid of creative imagination and a sense of genuine humanity is dead at the core. Only the worm remains."

"I didn't realize that it had gotten so bad," the physician said. "I've been gone a long time...."

The Austrian honored the long pause, then he continued with a crack of outrage in his voice. "Do you know that Himmier has been wanting to get rid of theater and art as we know it. He calls it *degenerate art*. That—from a degenerate like himself! I left not because I was afraid of being branded a Jew, but because I could no longer stay in a country that gives away its power to a low-life like that. Why, even rats have a better sense of life and living. They, at least, don't engineer the collective death of their own kind. What is worse still—the worm wants to suck out the life of the German soul and render it a deadened machine. No art, no literature, no history. Above all, no spirit."

The two men stayed sitting at the table for a long time without another word. They seemed to absorb each other's company like destitute children away from home soaking in the comfort of human contact. Then they got up, looked around with a kind of empty glance and proceeded to walk away, at first very slowly, then with a brisker pace toward a secondary road.

Meanwhile in New England, the father, seeing it was Friday night, went to the Sandy Bottom Saloon on lower Water Street to have a couple of beers and a chat with the boys. He occasionally went there to talk to his friends and some new acquaintances, like the fellow named Al from across the Twin City Bridge. The small saloon was a neighborhood drinking and meeting place where many of French ancestry joined in the weekly unburdening of worries, frustrations, and the tensions of hard work in a mill or a shop. Once in a while, one of the men would burst into song, and every now and then a chorus would be belted out with nostalgic gusto. The Irish had their own pubs and the Yankees their bars on the other side of town. Rare were the occasions when men crossed the bar boundaries. Rare also were the times when the men at the Sandy Bottom Saloon came to blows, even when drunk. Fighters would be escorted home by some of their comrades and delivered to the wife, who accepted the limp and merry-eyed husband with a grateful nod but not without muttering under her breath that a man of the house should not go spending good hard-earned money on binges. Besides, what would the neighbors think?

As the evening progressed, the father met this red-haired, red-eyebrowed chap who sang along, in French, with the other guys. His name was Daniel Patrick O'Mulray Garahan. He sang with a wisp of an Irish brogue that made his words lilt with the melody. He did not feel out of place with the rest of the men. No, sir, not with the Francoeurs, the Pelletiers, the Dubés, the Turcottes, the Simards, and the others. Why, he even had a sister who had married one of them, the hyphenated Americans who were as French as the Irish were Irish, he said. Of course, this kind of marriage was frowned upon by both ethnic groups, since the rule was no knotting among clans, as the Irish put it, or no mixed marriages, as the French declared it. But Daniel Patrick did not care about these things. He loved having fun and found it wherever he could, even if it was in a French neighborhood with his brother-in-law, Ti-Bé Lamontagne.

Sitting at the table with Gérard's father, Daniel Patrick began to talk to him with a slight slur of his speech, as the effect of the beer was now catching up with the movement of his tongue and lips. "You know, my friend," he said, "I should be your enemy. I come from the other side of the tracks. I'm Irish. Yesssssir, me name is Daniel Patrick O'Mulray Garahan of Dublin town and you're a frog-speaking French from the belle Quebeckeeee. You don't mind if I call you Frog, do you? You can call me *a tête-de-pioche maudit Irlandais* if you want .... son-of-a-bitch hardheaded Irishman. You know, if we let it all out once and for all, then there's no more enemy, no more fighting for nothing ... we are good Christian men and we want peace at work and at play, don't we now."

The father did not know exactly how to respond to such candid but humorous talk, and right to the core, too. "I'll tell you, *mon ami*," he said after thinking for a minute, "I really don't like to be called a frog by anyone, especially by those who want to make fun of me. But coming from you, I know that it's the beer that's doing the talking and it comes from the heart not the guts where anger grows and stews. As long as you don't call me Canuck. That means old farmer, dumb and backwards."

"Why do they call you frogs, anyway?"

"I don't know," the father replied. "Probably because the way we speak from the nose and the throat. It's a name that just seems to have stuck to us. I suppose it could have been a coon cat or beaver or *siffleux*, you know, a woodchuck. I haven't a clue. But I'll tell you, I just hate to be branded something that puts all of us in the same pocket. Sure we're French, but we're not all the same, just like you're Irish, but you're not like all of them.

"No, thank God! If they were all like me, Blessed St. Patty himself would turn over in his grave."

The two men laughed, and the others sitting around them joined in the laughter.

Ti-Gus Lajoie burst out of his lethargy by saying, "Hey, I hear that the Company men at Laconia Mills want to replace our men with some newly arrived Albanians. These foreigners are willing to work for lower wages. I hear that a few of them even sleep on cotton bales to save their money in order to send for their families. Cockroaches!"

One of the other men answered him, "Let's get them before we're sorry for letting this happen. I don't like foreigners, especially money-hungry ones."

"Just you wait a minute there, my friends," said Daniel Patrick. "We're all foreigners here. It just happens that we came here sooner. We're all in the same boat, all surviving as human beings."

"But," responded Ti-Gus, "we were here first. I was born in these here United States. We're more than these here Albanians."

"Why?" asked Daniel Patrick.

"Because," said Ti-Gus, "we're real Americans, We gotta protect our territory and our jobs. Those people just don't belong. I hear they don't even eat the same food as us. They're just plain outsiders. Let's pack 'em up and send 'em back where they belong. We'll put a big C on their asses, and kick the hell out of them. C for *Calvaire de Chiens!* Worthless dogs!"

The father sat motionless and silent while some of the guys snickered a bit but not in unison. Then a strange silence came over them like a fog rolling up over a hill and masking its sloping profile. Daniel Patrick looked sullenly at the father and made a fist with his right hand, cupping it with his left hand. One could see the weight of his hands, like the weapons of a fierce predator ready to strike. The father got up, put on his cap, and said, "I don't want to hear anymore of this talk. It chills my bones. Come on, Daniel Patrick. I'll take you home."

"Why?" the Irishman asked.

"Just because."

Back in the hamlet in Germany where the mother and the children were staying, Helmut was surveying the countryside. He was studying its tree-filled hills and deep inclines that rendered the hamlet practically invisible to the outside world. In here, Helmut felt invulnerable to the war that was going on out there. He knew that it existed, but somehow he didn't feel a part of it. Until now. Someone had been asking questions about Helmut. No one had asked him questions directly; all the questions about him had been directed to others. That frustrated him. It led him to believe there was a conspiracy about to be blown wide open. He was going to find out what was going on.

Helmut went to the Burgermeister and asked him point blank if he knew anything about this conspiracy.

"What conspiracy?" asked the astonished Herr Wurmerde.

"Why, the questions, the suspicion and the air of mistrust surrounding me in this village in the last few weeks."

"I know nothing of it," the Burgermeister flatly replied.

Helmut then decided to look into the matter himself. After all, he had been a true citizen of the *Reich*, a noble and trusted confidant of the authorities. True, he could not serve his country in a military way, but he nonetheless countered the enemy of his country by doing all in his power to help demolish them. It was indeed a complex situation for him, since the enemy did not have a face, not even a name. Just the French, the English, the Canadians, and, of course, the Americans.

Why did the Americans and the Canadians have to get involved again with the archenemy of the *Vaterland*, he asked himself. Hadn't they learned their lesson in the last war? So many still feeling the havoc of gas in their chest and bellies. That war had not been the least beneficial to anyone, he told himself. No victors, no losers, no just settlement, just plain craziness. All it had yielded were bodies, trenches that gouged the countryside, ever-deeper hatred, and the creation of the vermin that infected all of us as enemies, he soberly maintained, his mind set on finding out the reason behind things. "They're enemies of my country and we're enemies of theirs," he said out loud. Then, "I'm an enemy of peoples and lands that I don't even know about." Someone passing him and hearing him wonder out loud, smiled inquisitively at him. The stranger's look had been that of a puzzled, if not disgruntled, man.

At first, Helmut did not let the silent encounter bother him, but, after thinking a bit about it, what began to bother him was that fact that he did not know this man. He was a stranger in town. Helmut knew everyone and everyone knew Helmut. Who was this stranger? What was he doing here? Just passing through? Or was he one of those who were asking questions about him? Little by little, Helmut had become suspicious about this matter; now he was truly concerned. No, not concerned. Annoyed. And what truly annoyed him had been Herr Wurmerde's demeanor at the *Stadthaus*. He appeared to be dismissing him, as if he hadn't wanted to get involved. "An old friend getting rid of me just like that," Helmut said to himself. "Why, he had squirmed in his shoes appearing to be naïve about the whole thing." Helmut stopped short of returning to the *Stadthaus* and punching the man right on his mustache for lying to him. He knew he was lying. He also knew that if he did not stop this gnawing in his heart and soul, he would eventually be consumed by it, and then he could no longer be useful to his country. Now was a critical time for his country, what with talk about defeat and more suffering. This time, if he had anything to do about it, there would be a victor and Deutschland would overcome.

Meanwhile, in Switzerland, not far from the French and German frontiers, the physician and the Austrian were slowly finding their way to some kind of safety. Whatever safety was.

"Safety in time of warfare is anything that does not compromise your life," said the Austrian to the physician. "And as for freedom of movement, well one has to create his own."

They avoided any confrontation with officials. For fear of being captured, they skirted every center where people lived and congregated. They knew they were in a neutral country, but neutrality has a way of not being neutral all the time. For instance, they overheard that some Swiss officials did not always abide by neutrality when it came to Jews.

"When it comes to marginality," stated the Austrian, "people do not always respect the rules and the pledges. Marginalized people are always vulnerable to compromise and the dispensing of the rules."

"What do you mean by that," asked the physician.

"Well, look around you. Do you see many Jews running around freely in Switzerland? Do you see any Gypsies going about their business? How about yourself? A German and a good citizen who not only disagrees with his country but decides not to toil in the field of death and destruction. Now a nonconformist. A citizen without a valid passport. A truly marginalized citizen ... and look at me, too," he said. "A marginal number with marginal utility cast aside as a worthless Jew on account of my so-called questionable long-ago ancestry."

"They do what they want with you," responded the physician, "and if they have it in their mind that you do not fit in, well then, they make you fit on their huge Procrustean bed of conformed patriotism and racial idealism. Or you perish. Cut off. No room for irregularities."

Once, in a long stretch of woods out of reach and out of the way, the two men were able to relax and find sustenance for the night. They caught a hare with a piece of string, and while one was stripping the game of its skin, the other was busily making a fire. They roasted the hare on a wooden skewer fabricated with sticks. They laughed at the way some of the night birds came in close to their circle awaiting the remains of the roasting prey.

"Even the birds who usually sleep when it gets dark are feeling the bite of hunger," noted the Austrian.

"Everyone and everything seems to be affected by this war," the physician agreed. "It has turned things upside down. It's utter chaos for the world of people as well as that of animals. The animals must be wondering what the humans are doing to their world, mustn't they?" he asked. "Why, animals don't have enemies, even though some people talk of natural enemies such as the lion and the lamb or the dog and the cat. Animals have prey. It's the predator and the prey, if you wish, but no real enemies. No hatred. Only humans have enemies and wars. I suppose that comes about because animals don't have philosophies or ideals. They don't have to exercise control over others just to feel power."

"You're talking about misguided philosophies and ideals," said the Austrian. "We humans need ideals to soar above the heavens and link ourselves to the mysteries of life and creation. But some people misdirect ideals and send them plummeting into the depths of ego and darkness where the worm lives. They don't soar, they plunge. It's our very own downfall, we humans."

Deep darkness set in as they extinguished the fire, the darkness of the woods covering the muted life in the stillness of the night. Even the moon was hidden behind the clouds and the wind had died down so that stillness engulfed the woods as when a deep purple pall covers a hearse.

The two men held on to a guarded sleep for they had gotten used to sleeping cautiously, when the letting go is kept on hold and the eye is quick to open at any sign or noise that intrudes into the quietness of the surroundings. The physician was awakened by a bird trying to peck at the hare's carcass. He shooed the bird away, but he could not fall back to sleep. He stared into the darkness at the sky, where he imagined that one of the stars escaping the clouds was the home he had left. He imagined that he saw his son and daughter. How he missed them, these tiny humans. And his wife, where was she with the children? Surely she had run away from the strife of the war. But where? He had received only one of her letters, in which she announced to him that she was leaving Kassel on holiday with the children. Realizing that war letters are filled with cryptic messages, he had read between the lines that she was going away for quite a while, to a safer place, a place where the children would not be in harm's way. But where? What if she tried to reach him, now that he had escaped that hellish place? Dawn broke, and his companion awoke to find his friend sitting and staring at the sky.

The Austrian got up, rinsed his mouth with some water, passed his hand through his disheveled hair, and sat down by his companion. "It's time I told you my name," he said after awhile. "Because we are both stargazers, not enemies. My name is Amadeus Hermann Spiegel. *Loved by God*, my mother used to say. Sunday's child. I must say that I was cherished and at times spoiled. I learned to love the great outdoors where the light is so often clear, bright, and penetrating. Oh, those deep blue Vermeer skies absorb your intensity, your whole being just lying there on the hills. I'm not a man of the dark," he continued. "I hate gloomy skies and the darkness of night, when not even the moon and stars are there to render you solace. I was a being living with the luxury of time and carefree moments. This allowed me to nurture my imagination and my sense of creativity. My father, poor man, never quite understood me. Even at the university, I maintained my independence and my freedom not to do the conventional things. Like getting a job, any job. 'Why don't you settle down and find a meaningful existence for yourself?' my father kept asking me. But what is meaningfulness to youth? I didn't care for things, either. Just getting things because you can afford them. 'Idleness, pure idleness,' moaned my father."

The Austrian yawned and stretched, looking up at the blue sky. "I needed to set things straight in my mind," he continued. "That's all. Where was I going? I must admit that I strayed a bit too far with art and music. It completely took over my life. Art and music became my muses, the two things that settled my mind and my soul. There's something eternal, transcendental, about them. To this day, they are my paths to survival. I miss them, although I constantly relive both of them in my mind. It's my therapy against this mess of a war. The very worst thing about this war," he said, 'is that people like Hitler and Himmler go against the very grain of what it is to be a human being. They see foes everywhere and in everything that does not conform. Even in art and music. Their kind call it *degenerate art*. What is so regenerative or normal about not having any art? Or having a patterned, didactic art? In my book, art is not meant to channel, twist, grind, and coerce the mind, but to liberate it."

There was a long pause before the physician began to string his own story onto that of Herr Spiegel.

"I was born in Kassel," he stated. "My father was a physician. My grandfather was also a physician. I was expected to follow the tradition. Except, I didn't want to be a general practitioner. I wanted to become a surgeon. My name is Lukas Marchant. The name is Alsatian. Medical school really absorbs all of your time. I married my sweetheart, the only girl I truly knew and loved. Her name is Lotte I have two children. Morgen and Jenny. Jenny, I hardly got to know her before I was called to war. Both of my parents are dead. I have a sister who lives in Wittenberg. My wife's family moved to Sweden after the first war. She has no relatives in Germany except for a cousin who lives on a small farm in deep southern Germany." He paused, wondering where that farm was and who else lived on it. "I was sent to Italy to operate on wounded bodies," he continued. "My art had been in surgery, but I'm afraid after my experience down there, my sense of creativity has been battered into nothing but a nightmare. It's hard to be a pacifist at heart when the system doesn't allow for any deviance from the hard line of fascist ideals. I'm not prone to super-patriotism. I don't see lines between peoples, only questions about their behavior sometimes. We have a very rich Volk heritage, but, my God, do we have to stay in the dirt not just with our feet but with our heads, too, and not rise above the mounds of clay so that we may gaze at the stars?"

The Austrian responded with a beguiled smile. "We are a strange people," he said, "strange in a sense of estrangement in dealing with people."

"Tell me about your escape from Austria," said the physician.

"Well," the Austrian said with a sigh, "after my daughter found out about my questionable ancestry, she fell into a deep depression. She then started denouncing me to her friends and fellow workers, as if I were her enemy not her father. She completely disassociated herself from me. She even alienated her children from me, my only grandchildren. My son was in the military. I didn't know of his whereabouts. For all I know, he is dead. My three children—dead to me."

"My wife," he continued, "died of grief when our other son killed himself. He was such a tender child, an overly sensitive young man who could not absorb the cruelty of society. Like you, he was pacifist, a truly committed pacifist. He died for his ideals rather than submit to the call of the military, and so he got to be known as a coward. Even his courageous act of suicide was a signal to the townspeople that he was only a lowly coward. To the people, cowards are just like enemies. My wife and I had to live with the shame engendered by his actions. But I still carry it as a badge of honor. My wife could not take it. She shut herself up like a lonely moth with shame festering in her heart. After I was branded a Jew, what else could I do but escape? I said to myself, when will they come for me, the Gestapo? They were bound to come. Where could I go? There are several neutral countries, but when I started listing them with their advantages, I found only one where I thought I could save myself from the predators of marginal enemies. Spain has Franco. I could not abide by his regime. Portugal is a gateway to the United States, but this land of the free has already been shut off to Jewish refugees. There was Sweden, but I did not want to go north. Turkey. However, knowing its history of strife and conflict, I did not want to become a stranger in a land of east-west tensions. Argentina appealed to me, but, mark my word, that's where many of the fleeing high command will go when this mess is over. They're not going to hang around Europe. That left Switzerland, the initiator of the red J."

After another pause, the Austrian continued his story. "People think that Switzerland is truly neutral, but I soon found out that neutrality has its own limitations, if not priorities. Switzerland's priorities are gold and survival. That means collaborating with the war machine ... with the Gestapo. At the time, I was living with a friend near Bamberg. I took the train from Bamberg to Stuttgart, then on to Zurich, Bern, and my destination, Fribourg. You know, come to think of, it was on the train from Kassel to Bamberg, two years ago that I met this lady with her two children, Morgen and Jenny. They were heading south, the mother told me. I remember young Morgen, the most inquisitive child I have ever met."

"That's him!" cried out the physician. "My son! My family. How were they? Were they sad? Did they look afraid? Did they say where they were going?"

"Hold on, now," the Austrian said. "No, they did not seem afraid at all. The woman was reserved, but how could she not be guarded in this time of the watchful eye and ear? No, she didn't specify exactly where her destination was, except to say that she still had a good ways to go."

"South of Bamberg ... but who lives there?" The physician stood in deep concentration, making an effort to recall any friend or relative who could give his family safe haven. "A city away from it all," he said. 'No, even smaller, a village, perhaps. A farm the only one that comes to mind is that of Lotte's cousin, Sophie. But, my God—Lotte has never been close to her. It's a cousin on her mother's side and that side of the family was never close. Sophie is a true *volkswoman*, one of the ancient stock of landowners who cultivate the earth for its bounty. But, well, who knows? Lotte is ingenious enough to think things through. No one really knows about her Cousin Sophie, and this makes it almost foolproof when it comes to identifying friends or relatives who shelter people. Not a single one of her friends would know. Lotte never talked to anyone about Sophie."

"Where does she live?" asked the Austrian.

"A small village near the Swiss border," the physician replied. "I believe its name is Rotkohl." He took a step forward. "I've got to go there."

"And risk not only your life, but the lives of your wife and children?"

"I know, I know. But I have to go."

The Austrian laid a hand on his friend's arm. "First of all, we have to get out of here. It's not safe."

"What do you mean it's not safe?"

"It's not safe. Switzerland is not safe for Jews and people without a passport."

Herr Spiegel continued his story where he had been cut off, thus answering his friend's query about travel and safety by relating his own experiences in Switzerland.

"I chose Fribourg as my final destination," he said, "because it's a university center and as a former teacher of classical music, I was drawn to this old city. When I switched trains, I did not encounter many guards who checked papers. In Zürich, I avoided the station and kept myself out of the way. The station was very busy. The same thing in Bern. There are ways, you know, of being inconspicuous. However, once in Fribourg, I had to get out through the station. I was greeted by a young Swiss guard who asked me for my papers. I handed them over to him. He looked at them and scrutinized my passport. I knew he recognized the red J. He looked at me, looked at the passport, and looked at me again. I simply stared at him, seemingly unperturbed. At least, that's what my exterior showed, but inside I was scared. He motioned me to go to his left with some others who seemed to be detained for some reason or other. I tried to walk away, but another guard stopped me with his rifle. So much for neutrality, I said to myself. I wasn't a criminal, nor was I an enemy. Why was I being detained? 'You are not being detained,' the first guard assured me. 'We need to clear your papers.' 'But there's nothing wrong with my papers,' said I. 'You are a bit too arrogant, my good man,' shouted the young man. I knew that I was getting myself into trouble if I waged a war of words with this one. I coolly stepped back and did his bidding."

There were eight of us," he continued. "Seven red J's and one anonymous one. We waited for an hour. Nothing was happening. I started to believe that our safety was in peril, that our freedom of movement was in danger. There was something suspicious going on. But I dared not question the young guard. He was definitely following orders. Suddenly, I thought I saw three men in long leather coats passing by the train. I asked to go to the bathroom. The guard looked at me suspiciously, then waved in the direction of the WC. He knew I wasn't going far when I went to relieve myself, since my luggage was there at my feet. I had to get away. I knew it deep down inside of me. I closed the door of the WC and saw that the window was big enough to squeeze through. The window was stuck. I worked frantically to get it open. I didn't want to break the glass for fear of making any noise."

"I finally managed to lift it high enough so as to get my body through it," he continued. "I jumped out and ran. I don't think anybody saw me because the bathroom window was at the far side of the station and the outside was not lighted at all. I ran. I ran not knowing if I would fall into the hands of the police or even the Gestapo. I swear that the guards were waiting to hand us over to the Gestapo. Himmler's henchmen. They're everywhere. What's a few Jews to the Swiss if it means survival and being remuneratively collaborative?"

"That's when I came to the flophouse where I met you." Herr Spiegel laughed. "My great escape. Some escape. I thought I was going to find peace and freedom in a neutral country. Where to now? All I know is that I must move on until I find peace and freedom."

The two men walked slowly out of the woods and onto a narrow dirt road that led to a farmhouse. They walked along the side of the road being especially careful not to draw attention to themselves. They were hungry, they were cold, they were dirty, not having washed for the last two days. Being dirty can make anyone feel as if he no longer belongs to the human race, as if he is two rungs lower on the ladder of the human species, lower even than the realm of animals. Animals, at least, find ways of cleansing themselves, some with their own tongue and saliva. Somehow the human species has not found a way to imitate the animals. Humans have to depend on outside cleansing agents when available. Hunger and grime, the thieves of self-respect and human dignity.

The two companions skirted the road to approach the farmhouse by the backyard. They crouched down when they reached the porch, peering up to see if anyone was watching them. There wasn't a sound, only the far away noise of a woodcutter.

As they started to raise themselves up, carefully keeping their eyes on the door, the cold steel of a rifle barrel was introduced at the nape of the physician's neck. Both men froze. Herr Marchant suddenly realized that he had escaped only to meet his end in a deserted farm yard somewhere in Switzerland. He was so stunned that he could think of nothing, he could say nothing. He became like stone. His companion began to shake all over until he lost all control of his muscles. He couldn't even defend his companion from the sudden attack. He was like putty, weak and deprived of all vigor.

"Where are you two going?" a strong harsh voice asked. "Speak up or I'll turn you over to the authorities."

A slight hope crept into the two men's frozen minds. At least it wasn't the Gestapo or the police.

"Turn around," said the voice.

The two men turned. They came face to face with a tall, intense-eyed man whose lower lip protruded from his face. He was wearing old clothes. "Who are you and what are you doing here?" he demanded.

"We, we ... we are looking for shelter and food, that's all," responded the Austrian.

"I hope you're not thieves or runaway prisoners," said the man. "I can't stand that kind."

"No, no, no," said the physician, smiling as much as he dared. 'We are not that kind. We are running away only because we have nowhere to go. But we are not criminals."

And the Austrian was quick to add, " Please, sir, have mercy. We are the victims of our circumstances. We really would not want to fall into the hands of the Gestapo."

"The Gestapo? What do they have to do with the Swiss?"

"Well," the Austrian said slowly, "you may not know that some of your countrymen are collaborating with the Gestapo when it comes to the undesirables."

The man lowered his gun slightly. "I heard of that," he said after a minute, "but I never believed the stories I was told. Are you sure?"

"Yes, I'm sure," said the Austrian, "I saw it with my own eyes in Fribourg."

"Are you sure you're not out to do some evil deed?"

"My dear man," retorted the physician, "we are the ones to whom evil was done. We are the victims. We're not the enemy."

Then, since the man looked trustworthy and seemed sympathetic, the two companions revealed to him the details of their escape. Inviting them inside, he told them that he was a farmer who had lost his wife some years back and had no one left. After some of his friends invited him to participate in the liberation effort, he had joined the underground. Not that the Swiss needed liberating, he said, but he hated the *Boches* just as the French did. The pigs had killed his brother-in-law and his family because they had sheltered some French Jews in the town of Puy in France. Across the border. Puy, of course, had turned out to be a Gestapo stronghold. A cesspool of spies and informants, the resistance said, nurtured by the Vichy government.

"One of my nieces escaped all of this," he said, "because she had gone to Chambon for the weekend, where she stayed with a family named Fayolle. Le Chambon-sur-Lignon is a town of hill people, people who cultivate the earth. They are the descendants of the Huguenots, who themselves were persecuted in the sixteenth and seventeenth centuries. They are a strong people, a people who survived massacres and the revocation of all their rights. Although by unfortunate circumstances they became an enemy of their own co-citizens," the man added, taking some vegetables and a pot out of a cupboard, "they have remained a deeply moral people who ardently believe in the love of the other. *Aimez-vous les uns les autres* is inscribed on the lintel of their little church. I saw it myself when I visited Chambon once in 1942 when I crossed the border into France with the *maquis*.

"Chambon," he continued, beginning to chop the vegetables with his large knife, "is also a kind of small center for the forging of papers. They're good, too. High quality. One of the farmers hides them in beehives because he knows that the Gestapo or the Vichy officials, like Pétain's watchdog, Lamirand, will not go hunting for them in the hives. I believe the farmer's name is Héritier. I met him. Chambon-sur Lignon is a quiet, friendly, hardworking village that believes in itself, that its old values and strength of character will always live on. It endures. The Chambonais do not marginalize anyone. They believe strongly in the worth of the person as an individual. What is unusual about these people is the fact that what they do for the Jews puts them in grave danger, but they don't see that as being heroic. It's just their duty as fellow human beings, they say. What a model town for those who seek freedom! They don't play games with human lives. They seek no power. Very much different from the Vichy people. Power and treason, that's their game. Well, now that the German armies are being driven out, Pétain and his collaborators have fled to Germany. *Les cochons.*"

The man's efforts to help those in need had doubled when he had learned about the Gestapo breaking the "Comet" escape line in Brussels, which funneled the victims of Himmler's ideology from Belgium to Holland and then to the Pyrenees, where they could escape. That was in January of 1943, he told them. Now he realized that his own country had not been thoroughly neutral when it came to the marginal people, as they were called, especially the Jews with the red J on their passports. They could be spotted right away at any terminal or border crossing. He said that he tried to help those who came from France into Switzerland. He even had linked up to another escape route from Holland. In the village of Zelgate on the Belgian-Dutch border, he said, lived a good man by the name of John Weidner. He was a Dutch Seventh-Day Adventist who coordinated the escape line. Thanks to him, many got out from the clutches of the Gestapo before the liberation of Antwerp, two months ago.

"Can we go up the escape line from Switzerland to Holland from here?" asked the Austrian.

"Why?" responded the man. "You're safe here. You're in a small village called Bulle. No one will suspect you here."

"That's just it," Herr Spiegel said. "We may be safe in Bulle, but we're not free to go about. I have a red J passport and Herr Marchant has none. What can one do without papers?"

"We can probably get you some papers."

"Yes," countered the physician, "but we would still not be truly safe. Switzerland doesn't always play by the neutrality rules."

The man paused in his chopping and looked at the two strangers in his kitchen. "How do you know that I won't turn you in then?"

"Because, my friend, you had family members killed by the Gestapo and you're wearing a small fleur-de-lys on your shirt pocket. No true enemy of the hated ones would wear such an emblem, I think," said the Austrian.

"You're right," the man said. "I wear it for Chambon-sur- Lignon. You'll notice that I don't wear the Cross of Lorraine but the fleur-de-lys. The cross has been profaned by the Vichy."

"Who are you, really?" asked the physician.

"My name is Pierre Chabanel. I'm a lawyer. I used to teach jurisprudence at the University of Fribourg. I don't do much teaching nowadays. I prefer to be on my land and, like Voltaire, I cultivate my garden. That way, I don't have to follow any political line. I work on my farm."

"And you work underground," said the physician.

"Oh, that's just *mon honnête* bêtise," replied the lawyer.

Back in New England, the latest news was that Maggie Létendre had been caught with a guy selling stolen goods. Maggie Létendre was the so-called bad girl of the neighborhood. She had always gotten into messes, even as a child. Nobody liked her. She managed to twist and change any affection anyone developed for her into feelings of apprehension and dislike. She was even alienated from her family. The only one for whom she showed any slight feelings was Tony Santa Lucia, a bad-luck kid from the other side of town. Maggie and Tony were made up of the same stuff, people said. They were both like mattress stuffing, nice to sleep on but worthless and made to be hidden away. Well, Maggie got pregnant by Tony. They were both sixteen, both out of school and out of work. Out-of-wedlock pregnancy was tantamount to crime. It made a girl an outcast. It brought shame, not only to the girl but to the entire family. The entire neighborhood, if not the whole of the Little Canada, where she lived, suffered the shame. People whispered more, they looked down when any mention was made of Maggie. People avoided the family and made it known in the not too subtle ways of shame gatherers that they intended to disassociate themselves from the sin of the woman. Maggie's sin. Oh, yes, the people said, it was less Tony's sin than the sin of the pregnant one who allowed herself to be put in that way. She was not only the fallen girl. She was the lost girl.

So Maggie, pregnant and now a thief, was sent away to an institution, La Maison Lacordaire. There they allowed her to think about her past and her shame. Tony moved away. She received no visitors. Gérard's mother was the only one not to spread the ugly rumors that Maggie had tried to abort her baby but failed. Gérard's mother sometimes sneaked out and offered the nuns a generous donation for the poor so she would be let in to see Maggie. After all, Maggie was the daughter of her best friend, Mrs. Denoncourt.

When Maggie delivered the child, it was quickly put up for adoption. A couple from Central Falls, Rhode Island, took the baby home. Maggie's family did not even want to see it. "Let her get out of her own mess," they said. "It's nothing but a child of shame." When Gérard's mother finally went to visit Maggie after the delivery, she learned that the nuns had given Maggie a hard time at the delivery. The doctor had been summoned, but he was late. In the meantime, one of the nuns had pushed back the baby's head and said out loud to the soon-to-be mother who had received no anesthetic that it was God's will that such a person suffer for her shame. Maggie had screamed until another nurse had put her hand tightly over Maggie's mouth. When the doctor finally arrived, the birth was completed.

Gérard's mother told Maggie's mother about the delivery, though she did not want to hear about it. "But, it's your own child," she cried out to Mrs. Denoncourt. "Don't you have any love or any feelings at all for her and your very own grandchild?"

"I have no feelings for people who bring shame to others and let them become the laughing stock," Maggie's mother shouted back. "Don't you know that we have to live with that?"

"But, it's your own flesh and blood. Your daughter. Not your enemy."

"Let her live with it."

That was the day Gérard's mother stopped visiting her closest friend. Maggie's mother likewise avoided Gérard's family altogether and especially prohibited her son, Clement, from playing baseball with Gérard. Gérard took this hard, since he and Clem were a team, he the catcher and Clem the pitcher. They always had played together. Soon Gérard's other friends began to taunt him for splitting up with Clem and, what was worse, he was deemed responsible for losing so many games now. "Shame on Gérard," they said.

Meantime, in the hamlet where the mother, the children and Cousin Sophie lived, a momentous occasion had arrived for the townspeople. Cousin Sophie was to be decorated for her virtues as a woman of the *Volk*, hardworking, tenacious, and enduring. Just like the soil of the Deutschland. A model of a woman, the authorities said. She, like the people, will live on and prosper. No enemy, no forces, no ill-fate can obliterate such people.

Sophie Dunkelntappen had lived in the hamlet for sixty-three years. She was sturdy and strong of character and constitution. She was one of the many peasants whose body had become accustomed to large amounts of potatoes, cabbage, and bread, and her body had overcompensated for the large intake of starchy foods by creating huge rounded lumps of fat, here and there, like an old tree sprouting unsightly knobs. Cousin Sophie also liked inordinately large portions of pancakes and *Kuchen*, which had, so they said, at length contributed to her stultification. But others insisted that she was born that way, slow and simpleminded with a tendency to be fleshy. She had never been outside her farmland, except once when she had ventured to a fair at Blauen. She had never married, never known the sweetness of romance nor the tenderness of a child. Her calloused hands were her badge of duty mixed with unwavering patriotism. However, if the eyes are the window of the soul, her pale blue, lusterless eyes did not in any way reveal any inner movement nor intimate any deep feeling.

The officials of the hamlet gathered in the town hall, where they ceremoniously received the delegate from the Reich headquarters. He was stiff, cold in his bearing and meticulously correct in speech and gesture. Cousin Sophie was dressed in her Sunday best, wearing also a thin smile that reminded one of the sheep she kept. Banal in its display and remarkable for its expanse, the smile remained fixed like the lips on a huge mask. The medal suspended from a blue and yellow ribbon was draped over the woman's chest. She bowed and the delegate executed a Nazi salute. Everyone in the room followed by shouting *Heil Hitler.* A common wine was served and everyone came to congratulate Sophie. She bathed in her moment of glory like an ungainly child who doesn't know what to do when faced with activity that gives one goose flesh all over.

The mother and the children had stayed home because the mother believed that they had better not go and be noticed. They would, she said to the children, have their own celebration afterwards. But Helmut was there in the town hall waiting to gain the delegate's attention, although he was now hesitant about being with a group of town officials whom he no longer trusted due to the suspicion thrust upon him. Cousin Sophie had looked at him askance, but without too much attention, as if she had wanted not to notice him at all. As if he were an embarrassment, he told himself. Well, he didn't care, he never liked the old sow, anyway. She always gave him the shivers, what with her rustic manners, her strange aloofness, and especially her voracious appetite. Why, she could devour an entire meal in no time and then ask for more. For him, she was a hollow person, in mind and spirit, with a bottomless pit for a stomach at that.

Helmut sensed that Sophie did not like her cousin spending so much time with him. He knew that she had neither any appreciation for nor any cognizance of the fine arts. She loved the official art of

Adolph Wissel and Julius Paul Junghanns, for she admired what was called their pictures of simple country life" as part of the "blood and soil' philosophy. Although Helmut never dared to divulge his true feelings about it since he feared a reprimand from the official voice. He detested this parody of art. Intellectually, he recognized the value of the peasant and the union with the soil, but he could not identify with the brutish people who represented this so-called natural life. They repulsed him. But he took refuge in the ideology of the Reich, of Aryan ideals, of the forthright determination to overcome the enemy and the promise of a new millennium with its superiority of will.

Rumors were that Helmut was a Gypsy. A worthless Rom with no real roots. Someone, they said, had researched Helmut's background and discovered that he did not belong. Neither to the nation nor to the land, certainly not to the people. He was a *marginal being.* Worse, he had become an undesirable in the minds of many who now perceived the matter as undeniable truth even though nothing had been proven. Besides, he was considered to be unqualified for military service, and now even the Gestapo was starting to ask questions about him. Wasn't that the true mark of his being some kind of reprobate? Finally, the boil of suspicion had festered long enough and the pus-filled swelling had burst wide open and its discharge was now spreading through town. Helmut was the enemy of the people. The enemy of the moment. It seemed that everyone wanted him out, if not dead. There was talk of reporting him to the high command. The Burgermeister, however, did not want any fanfare about this. He feared some kind of bad publicity and wanted no destructive criticism laid on the town. Helmut wasn't worth it, he said, so a committee was formed to handle this affair.

Before the committee had even begun to deliberate, however, Helmut was gone. Vanished. He had one last brief meeting with the mother in the shady grove behind the huge oak tree where they sometimes met. He said his farewell despondently. He didn't want to endanger her and her children by letting her know of his destination. He had so wanted to be part of the Reich movement, he told her, and now all hope had been dashed by some silly rumors. Who would want to ruin the life of a lame but zealous patriot, he had asked her. He left her with a look in his eyes that was penetrating, lucid, and at the same time pathetic.

"I embody all that the Third Reich detests and wants to eradicate," he said. "Racial and social pollution. I'm part Rom, a cripple, a dark-skinned pervert, a homosexual. I'm caught in the web of my fate. You didn't know all that about me. I didn't mean to hide things from you. I wanted to protect you from this while keeping my own sense of dignity."

All she could do was to look in his sad eyes and feel his pain.

The lawyer, Pierre Chabanel, was ready. He was able to reach Holland and talk to his contacts about the escape of the two men under his charge who wanted to get out of Switzerland and the proximity of Germany. Herr Spiegel had a shattering nightmare the night before they left. He dreamt that his daughter had shot him point blank with a pistol while he escaped through Germany. Her children, hollow-eyed, watched the killing and could not move. Their feet were ineradicably meshed into the ground, and their uplifted arms and hands were like the rot of decaying bark while their pale hair floated colorlessly in the blinding light. Their voices sounded like distorted trumpets whose blaring sound was hauntingly strained. Everything had occurred in slow motion so that all of the violence and madness of the drama were heightened beyond measure. He knew that it was indeed time to flee from this space that haunted him like a specter.

The physician, Herr Marchant, looked back at the farmyard as he hurried to catch up with his friends. He could not put out of his mind the vision of returning home, not to Kassel, but to the quiet farm where his family had found shelter. He was sure now that was the place his wife had gone to. He saw himself going in circles, however, trying almost in vain to reach home. Some kind of home. But where was home now? Would there be a home? Could he and his family start over again? In peace and freedom?

"Come on!" shouted Pierre "Hurry, or we'll be late to catch the cargo wagon that's waiting for you."

The physician was cold. It was late December and the wind was biting. He clutched his new passport in his pocket like a child holding on to his last toy. Herr Spiegel followed him. They were two men in the wind being blown here and there by their fortune or rather, misfortune.

CHAPTER SIX

The ride on the cargo van was long and arduous. There were bumps in the road. Darkness surrounded the two hidden men, who had to endure the stifling odor of rotting canvas on their bodies and the constant fear enveloping them. It seemed to them that they had zigzagged back and forth across the border of Germany and France, always keeping on the bumpy, narrow, country roads. The network planning the escape had chosen the Christmas holiday, figuring that people would be too busy and too caught up with the seasonal celebrations, or at least with the keeping of Christmas, to pay much attention to an old cargo van straggling along at night on out-of-the way roads. The driver was used to this long run, he had done it time and time again, shuttling the marginal ones from borderline safety to sometimes more precarious harbors. At least away from the enemy of those fleeing from the far-reaching net of the Gestapo. Himmler knew and prided himself that the Gestapo always got their man like a hunt in which, no matter the obstacles, the prey would always be caught. There was no escape, Himmler liked to tell himself. After all, he was in control. Total control.

Herr Marchant and Herr Spiegel were trapped in a bulbous hollow space under the van that had served as an escape container for countless victims of the Nazi plot led by Himmler to strip Germany, if not all of Europe, of the blight of the unwanted and the undesirables. The men felt cramped and somewhat claustrophobic in the dark belly of the vehicle, but at the same time they felt happy that, at last, they were going to taste freedom. Herr Marchant wondered if he still knew what freedom was, but then he caught himself in his doubts and quickly realized that, of course, freedom was what it was all about. It meant free to be yourself, free to be with your family, free to have friends no matter who they were. Free like the wind in the meadow that scurries through the flowers, the grasses and even the unwanted growths people called weeds. Free was not having to go against your principles. Freedom was not having wars, enemies, not fearing the clutch of the Gestapo. Freedom? Well freedom is, that's all.

They had been told not to speak, at least stick to brief, bare whispers, but at times the urge to talk was stronger than the admonition. Yes, they had to remember that safety was first and foremost, but after some hundred miles or so, like Jonah, the men wanted to burst out of the belly of the whale. After all, human beings were meant for the open spaces where one can breathe the night air and take in the variety of scents and smells that comforted them or warned them about the presence of cities and towns nearby. They were told by the driver, during a brief rest out of the hollow of the van, that they had reached Valentigny and they were next going to Fontaine, where the driver would be changed. At Fontaine, some ninety kilometers from Mulhouse, the cargo was also changed from hay and vegetables to faggots and cabbages. Herr Marchant grabbed a cabbage from a crate and hungrily ate some of the reddish leaves, offering them also to his companion.

The driver left Fontaine and headed for Benfeld, avoiding, at all cost, the vicinity of Strasbourg. It was at Puttelange that he warned the hidden men to be on their guard. He was going to leave them at Marmoutier near Saverne and another driver, a Dutchman, would take over. Saverne was full of Gestapo agents and he would try to go around the city and meet his replacement under an old bridge where only a trickle of water could be heard.

The night was cold, very cold and the sky was without stars. As the cargo van maneuvered the many curves in the road and came to a crossroad where the driver knew he had to take a left, two armed men appeared on the side of the road as if they had come out of nowhere.

"Good God, the Gestapo," the driver muttered, knowing full well that his route had been, all along, a dangerous one. At every stage of the escape route he had given thanks that he had not come face to face with the Gestapo. But now he was caught what with two escapees in the belly of his van. He stopped the van, turned off the switch, and waited for the armed men to make their first move.

Out of the van," one shouted. He obeyed. The other started to probe here and there and then pushed aside the large tarpaulin covering the back of the van. He stuck his rifle into the cargo of cabbages and fired several shots. The two men inside the bowels of the van were frozen with fear. One of the bullets grazed the physician's arm and he felt the blood trickling down his sleeve. Then, one agent went under the van, stretched himself out on his back and looked at the underside as if he already expected to find something hidden. He came back up, brushed his clothing and announced that he had found what he was looking for. The driver stood motionless. His eyes were fixed on the ground and he dared not stir. He knew he could do nothing to help the two men. He felt he had let the whole network down.

"What have you got in the cavity?" asked one of the agents with a cold stare.

"Nothing," answered the driver. 'It's a storage place for my tools."

"Well, let's see what you've got there."

The one who had been guarding the driver pushed him until they came to the back of the van. He made him empty the cargo and then he shouted with an angry voice, "Come out of there instantly or we will shoot." Nothing stirred. The other agent then shot a round next to the cavity. Suddenly a door at the bottom of the van opened and two heads appeared.

"There they are, my two rabbits," said the agent who had spotted the bulge under the van.

"Come out of there and let us see your filthy faces. We have places for you, scum Jews."

"But I am not a Jew," replied the physician.

"Who are you?" said the agent, standing face to face with Herr Marchant.

"I'm a German citizen and so is my friend."

"Traitors then." The Gestapo agent shoved Herr Spiegel to the ground.

"Shoot us and let's be done with it," replied the Austrian.

"Oh no, we don't relieve the undesirables like that. We have to go through procedures."

After they had searched all three men, one of the agents took the driver aside, made him kneel in front of him, and with a sudden thrust of his pistol shot the driver in the head. The two companions shuddered with mortal anticipation. Was this to be the end of it all for them?

As they were being led away by the Gestapo, there was a sudden thump beside the road. All the two fugitives could see were the dark forms of three men, who came swooping down like black falcons on the Gestapo agents. With swift and adroit maneuvers, a throat was slit and a heart was stabbed. The two fugitives had no idea now what to do, even though they understood that their fear of being slaughtered had been dispelled. Worse, they'd had visions of being taken away to a death camp where they would join thousands of skeletal men and women waiting for their death.

"We are partisans," said one of the men who had carried out the rescue. "We don't have time to explain. You must be on your way again. We were expecting you. We serve as part of a team of escape monitors along the escape route. The Gestapo are everywhere. They sense that they are being fractured while the whole system is falling apart. Many have concentrated on this area. Your driver, of course, did not know that."

The movements of the three men were swift and without wasted effort. One of them picked up the lifeless body of the slain driver and slung it over his shoulders. Blood spilled over his back as he scurried to join another partisan in the shadow of a tree. Both of them disappeared into the darkness while one of the other men helped the two companions back into the cavity. He didn't take the time to reload the cargo. He switched on the engine and pushed on the accelerator with his right foot so hard that the vehicle started to shake and choke. The new driver got the vehicle under control and the two fugitives were headed for the last leg of the escape route.

After an hour or so, the vehicle stopped again and yet another driver was substituted. He was Dutch and moved with careful gestures. What about the partisan who had helped them out of the mess back there? There were to be no goodbyes, no chatting, the new driver told them. It meant the safety of the partisan as well as theirs. Everything had to be done with utmost silence, efficiency, and speed. They were given a few minutes to stretch and to look up at the night sky. Herr Spiegel asked his companion if he did not want to go for it, meaning leave this dark transport since the escape was gnawing at his entrails like a bad meal gone undigested.

"Where would we go, my friend?" his companion asked.

"Out there," replied Herr Spiegel.

"But out there, that's where the temptation of freedom is, I'm sure. If we go out there, we will again become the hunted with nowhere to go. Real freedom is not running away. Besides, if we run away, we'll be facing certain death."

"Sometimes I wonder which is worse, death or this living agony of being no one nowhere."

"Come, my dear friend," said the other, "we will both do it together. Let's soar in the dark like stars. Let's not become rotten fruit that falls to the ground."

The van wended its way through Luxembourg then into Belgium. The way seemed endless, as endless as pain that won't go away. The two men had no idea where they were. For all they knew, they could still be in France, or even Switzerland, so weary were their minds and so worn out their bodies. The journey had become a nightmare. The two men started to fantasize about their bodies floating ever upwards, their heads turning into heavy sponges soaking in the rain they heard beating on the vehicle. Their eyes were wide open but in the darkness of the van they saw nothing until they began to hallucinate. Then they saw all kinds of things—hares, spiders, monkeys, tigers, reptiles, tall grasses, moonlight caught in the web of the syrupy tissues of their flesh, waking thoughts stuck in the mesmerizing but dagger-like entrapment of barbed wire, hollow eyes staring at them through floorboards where the undesirables slept in the cold. They felt empty, void of any feelings or even the ability to feel. As hollow as reeds, as empty as the dried-up peelings of fruit. After a while, they finally fell asleep. A soft voice roused them. It was the driver telling them that they were approaching Ghent and that they would soon reach Zelgate, right on the Belgian border. Finally, they would get a taste of safety. They were on the border of the Netherlands, which had been liberated a few weeks ago by the British.

Zelgate was one of the escape centers. This center was coordinated by John Weidner, known by all who worked with him as "the man with the glory eyes." Zelgate wasn't even on the map for those who didn't know how to look for it. Some two thousand inhabitants, that's all it boasted, a few horses, some stray cats and dogs, a rather quiet town. But Zelgate was known by all those who worked the escape routes. When one closed, another opened up. John Weidner and his stronghold of liberators had put much effort into their route. From Holland to Switzerland and from Switzerland to Holland, where the escapees went on to other, possibly freer spaces. On their own or linked to other routes, but not all of them safe and free from the clenches of the Gestapo, though. Take Gurs in the Pyrenees, for instance. This French camp for German refugees had been turned over to the Gestapo by the Vichy government. So often did the price of freedom come at great cost. But what could marginal enemies do?

Paris had been liberated in August, Antwerp in October, followed by Holland. Soon Europe would be rid of the crushing tyranny of the Nazis and freedom would be restored. Christmas 1944 had been a very good Christmas indeed. Now, at least, things weren't as difficult as before, said the Dutch, when the enemy was always at your heels and fear was constantly in your throat. Soon, very soon, it would be Himmler's turn to flee, some people said, since there was talk that the Reich was falling fast. The cat would become the mouse, some said.

Meanwhile, back at Rotkohl, Cousin Sophie was busy sewing Nazi patches of red and black on all of her clothing. She liked wearing her medal and all of the paraphernalia given to her by the party and she wanted more. She'd had the notion of giving herself entirely to the cause for quite some time now, and she began by wanting to wear all of her clothes that showed the sign of her zeal. Soon she was caught trying to read Nazi propaganda for which she had never shown any inclination. She had even said, at one time, that she despised such goings on. After accumulating piles and piles of materials that she collected at the Burgermeister's, her eyes grew bold and intense. Why, she was even seen discussing political matters on the square rather than working in the fields. She had become, indeed, one of the party faithful, and she displayed fits of intolerance for the slightest irregularities, like the way old Herr Schumlinger was too slow at removing his hat during the raising of the official colors. She even snapped at the children when they didn't register enthusiastic support for the party line, which, to her, stood for steadfastness, tradition, progress, and being part of the whole. The children thought she was weirder than ever.

Their mother had begun keeping her distance from her cousin. She didn't like the change that had come over Cousin Sophie. Sophie Dunkelntappen had become wild-eyed, her gait now resembled the Nazi goose-step. The mother feared for her children's safety and began to wonder how she could manage to escape from the farm. But where to go?

One Saturday in early March, when the thaw had melted pretty much all of the snow on the ground, Cousin Sophie came into the house very much disturbed that a deep and wide hole had dug itself in the fallow part of her garden. How was she to handle this gaping hole? She just couldn't just leave it like that, she told the mother, because she was afraid that someone might injure himself, especially at night, by falling into it. She was afraid that it would keep widening and harm her future crop. The mother replied that no one went out there in early March and that the matter could be handled later on when the ground would be more manageable. She assured Cousin

Sophie that old man Zerblutter, her neighbor, would certainly offer his help. That calmed Cousin Sophie.

The next week, Cousin Sophie stayed in bed for two days, saying that a bad cold had gotten the best of her. The mother wanted to call the physician. Sophie said no. The mother became edgy, She was now convinced that her old cousin was spying on her. But why? The children swore that Cousin Sophie watched them from her windows and ducked behind the curtains when she felt that she could see them watching her watching them. Something was going on, the mother was sure of it. She decided to take her children with her to talk to the local pastor. She would have to be very careful how she handled this matter. When she returned, Cousin Sophie couldn't be found. The mother searched every room in the house. Suddenly she heard a scream. It came from the barn. The mother ran until her legs were about ready to give up, and when she opened the barn doors, she found Cousin Sophie wielding a large knife in one hand and holding Jenny by the other.

"The enemy, the enemy is with us," Sophie blurted out in a forceful but shattered voice.

"But the enemy is not us, dear Sophie."

"It's everybody who stands apart from the party, who will not support the party, who will never be able to be part of the whole."

"We are part of the whole."

"No you are not! You are part of them, the outsiders.... I need to cleanse all of them ... all of you."

And with a voice that echoed the lost look in her eyes, Sophie pronounced, "The girl needs to be sacrificed for the good of the party for she is too young for the *Lebensborn* program. She cannot give the Führer a child, a true Aryan child who will one day become part of the whole. And the boy ... yes, the boy ... he must join the German army ... they are enrolling them now what dreams of glory, what great gift to the *Vaterland*. I want to help create the whole by tearing down the unwanted leeches that are dragging us down ... the *Volk* ... and the worms that are eating at our roots. Our land wants it so..."

The mother tried to approach Cousin Sophie, but the older

woman would have none of it. The mother tried to persuade her to drop the knife, but Sophie insisted that she had had a vision in which she was asked to sacrifice one for the many.

"Take me, not her," pleaded the mother.

Then, slowly but deliberately, a shotgun barrel appeared in the dim light of the barn. It wobbled a bit, but it was aimed straight at the frenzied old cousin. Morgen held the stock in his two hands with his right hand index pressed on the trigger. His voice was shaking. "I'm afraid," he shouted. "I'm afraid, but I can pull the trigger. I'm not a murderer. Please don't make me one let us go away from here. We'll leave you in peace with your ideas and your land."

"No," shouted Cousin Sophie, "I must do my duty." She lunged at the mother.

The gun went off straight at Cousin Sophie's head. Her face exploded in blood and bone fragments. As she dropped to the floor, the gun clanged on the edge of the milk can. Morgen had let go without knowing what he was doing. The mother ran to her daughter who wept and howled in her fear. Morgen just stood there, shaken. He had become like stone.

Within a few moments, the mother gathered her wits about her and was able to plan every step to be taken. She had to do it all, there was no one to help her. Once the children had been calmed down and were able to help with the tasks at hand, everything moved with swiftness and efficiency. First the body. They had to bury it, but with a certain amount of dignity; after all Sophie was a human being. As soon as darkness fell, they found the hole in the garden and managed to throw the body, wrapped in a white shroud, into it. It must have been four or five feet deep. Then, since the ground was still frozen, they carted manure and compost to fill up the hole. The mother said a few silent prayers, and they returned to the house. They all went to sleep in the same room, completely exhausted. The following morning they cleaned the barn and went to see the Burgermeister.

The mother reported that Cousin Sophie had left the village with just a few belongings. She wanted to be part of the action in the Berlin area, the mother said. She had taken her medal, her propaganda, and her official flag with her, the mother continued. She was sure that Cousin Sophie would reappear someday, but for now the old peasant was doing what she most desperately wanted to do, offer her life to the party. The Burgermeister said he understood such devotion and that he wished he could do the same. The mother and the children left his office quietly and headed for the farm. Would they stay there now that the farm was stained with blood, asked Morgen. But of course, the mother replied. It was the only place where they could be and, besides, father would eventually find them. She was sure of that. The blood was that of some other woman, she said, not Cousin Sophie. She did not know that other woman, the one who wanted to kill her children for the party.

"What you did was done in defense of self and of others, my son, and that is justified killing.

"Justified killing?" asked Morgen.

"Yes, it is supported by all that is just and right in this world. Ironically," she said, the Nazis, and all of their enemies kill because they think that it's justified, too. Who is right and who is wrong in all of this? Everyone has his own cause. All I know is that you did it to save others, not just to kill. She was not your enemy ... just a deranged poor old woman who listened to the voices of darkness."

It was thus decided that the family would stay on the farm and wait for father.

In the neighborhood where Gérard lived, the news was that Pitou Blanchette had killed his sweetheart's lover. He wasn't a killer, certainly, not a bad guy, he didn't have an enemy in the world. Everyone liked Pitou. But he had a bad streak of jealousy in him. When he found the man in bed with his girlfriend, Pitou went mad, berserk. The other man had laughed at him. That made Pitou crazy. He shot him, point blank. Then he dropped the gun. The police had come, two cars full. There was an investigation. It was all the neighborhood talked about for weeks on end. Just like the movies, thought Gérard. Of course, he didn't know all the details, but he gathered some of them as the grown-ups talked about the event. Gérard thought it strange that the neighbors talked about the dead man like he was a complete stranger, an outsider, an enemy. Why, he lived right across the way in the next neighborhood. But he just didn't belong there. He'd come to the neighborhood to stir up trouble. After all, it wasn't really Pitou's fault if he couldn't contain his anger and jealousy. It was the other guy's fault. He meddled. He didn't belong. That's what you get when you intrude, they said. But did Mr. Blanchette have to kill him? young Gérard asked silently, staring at the ceiling in his room. Then he got up, put on his baseball jacket, and went out to play with his friends.

A week passed. Gérard was mad. He had never been so mad. Someone had stolen his bag of prized marbles. He always kept a keen eye on them, never letting them out of his sight. After all, he had won them fairly and with great skill. He was awfully proud of his bag of marbles, and now they were gone. Someone had taken them, he said. His mother had searched all over the house. She'd even interrupted her spring cleaning to search for them, so desperate was her son to find them. Every member of the household was affected by the loss of the marbles. Everyone felt the upheaval of something gone wrong even if it was only about a bag of marbles.

"Only a bag of marbles?" cried out Gérard to his sister. "Why, it's my bag and my collection that was taken away. It's a violation! An unfair thing was committed," he said with righteous indignation.

"All right, Gérard," his mother said. "I'll buy you some marbles if that will stop you from turning everyone's lives upside down."

"But I don't want just any old marbles," the boy protested. "I want what is mine. I won them, fair and square. I won them during the war of marbles at school. Someone took what is mine. I'll get them back. If it takes days, weeks, and months, I'll get them back and I'll get the one who stole them, and then I'll punch him in the nose."

"How do you know someone took them?" his mother asked. "Maybe you left them somewhere."

"I *know* someone took them. I never would leave them anywhere."

"Do what you have to do," his mother said, 'but stop annoying everyone about a bag of marbles. Go on, you'll be late for school."

Gérard left the house, disgruntled and angry with his mother.

"What does she know about marbles and winning," he asked under his breath.

The bag of marbles was found that very Monday morning. It was neatly lodged in Gérard's desk, right under his notebook, which he had forgotten. All weekend long, he hadn't been able to do his homework because his notes were in his desk under a bag of marbles. The matter was quickly dispelled and never spoken about again. People around Gérard were relieved.

People in Holland still felt deeply about the recent firestorm in Dresden, where some fires, it was reported, had lasted as long as seven days. A heritage city where they made beautiful things had been destroyed for the war. The allies had targeted it for tactical purposes not just because it was an enemy city. All that the people knew, everywhere in Europe, was that the bombing had been a horrible thing.

"There is always a sacrificial lamb in all of human undertakings," said Herr Spiegel, and Herr Marchant simply nodded his head.

"But Dresden of all places," continued the Austrian, "a city of creative art and genius, a living heritage. Why did the British have to sacrifice Dresden in their war effort to defeat the enemy? After all, there is such a thing as beauty. Beauty has worth over and above strategic importance."

People, it seemed, became more and more resigned to the facts of war, to its destruction and the upsurge of so many homeless, wandering people. What about those in the death camps? What about the children? The slaughter of sacrificial lambs was not over yet. Himmler had seen to it that the war would not only be marked in people's hearts but encrusted in their bowels as well, where deep in every crevice lay hidden secrets and worms.

April arrived in the Netherlands with the force of a giant, whipping its tail of winds and shedding torrents of rain. But in May the wind and the rain were soon replaced by soft breezes and the sweet scents of freshness and light. The two fugitives were now in Holland, living in a quiet city called Assen, up north where John Weidner had some close friends. They were resting, anticipating the next move. It was early May and the Reich was falling, disintegrating fast. Himmler was on the run.

Herr Spiegel was bewildered, if not torn, by the many suggestions people offered him about relocating himself. He flatly refused to go to Palestine, even though a new state was promised to those who were building the Jewish community. The diaspora was coming to an end, they said. At the very least the sowing to the wind was diminishing and the sons and daughters of Abraham were returning to the promised land.

"But I don't belong there," he kept answering these people. "I'm not really Jewish. I'm landless. Homeless and alone. Where can I go except to my dear Austria? Austria in ruins with no one there to receive me."

"But you can come with me," said his friend, Herr Marchant. "You can have a home with us. My family will surely receive you and welcome you."

The Austrian refused the offer. He didn't want to be in the way. He was looking for his own place, for his own identity. After all, he was someone even if the Reich had stripped him of all that seemed to matter in his life. He fell into a deep melancholy and would not talk for days. He wandered about listlessly.

A few days later, on May 19, Herr Marchant told his friend that he was going in search of his family and that he truly wanted him to accompany him. "Then, on the way," the physician told him, "if you find that you want to leave me and stay wherever you may want to stay, I will understand. But you simply cannot go on moping all day. Trust me, you will find a place."

And so the two men crossed the German lines and went on their quest for home. They didn't worry too much about the Gestapo anymore. Its leader was on the run. Everybody was on the run, it seemed. The two fugitives just didn't care. They were tired of being on the run and at the mercy of circumstances. They first went to Papenburg, then on to Bremen where they stayed for one day.

On May 23, they arrived in Lüneburg in northern Germany, where they were greeted by Dr. Luftkirche, an old friend of the

Marchant family. British General Montgomery had earlier accepted the surrender of all German forces in northwest Germany, Holland, the Islands, and Denmark. The surrender had been signed by Admiral Friedberg in Lüneburg. The talk of the town, however, was that Himmler had been captured at Bremervörde and brought to Lüneburg, where they had stripped him and searched him and made him ready for transfer. He had managed somehow to conceal a capsule of cyanide in his mouth, which he bit and died instantly, thus cheating the British of their fair game. It was also reported that Himmler had, in late April, met with Count Bernadotte of the Red Cross to negotiate capitulation. Himmler had offered to surrender but only to the Western Allies, not to the Russians, of whom he had a mortal fear. The Western response had been one of unconditional surrender, so Himmler had disguised himself, gone on the run, and wound up in the enemy's hands at Bremervörde after someone had found his papers to be suspicious. The master of papers and cataloguing had been given away by his own handiwork.

Herr Spiegel and Herr Marchant did not wish to view Himmler's body. So many people had rushed to see the Reichführer's remains, even though the British had forbidden it. The two men wanted to forget this being, this demonic little man who created the Gestapo and sent to their deaths so many victims who had become, not by their own doing, enemies of the Third Reich. As the war dragged on to its final stages, more and more was being divulged about the plight of the Jews and the Gypsies. The Reich had been in the business of building death camps for many months, even years, and filling the camps with men, women, and even children. *Children*—as unwanted, as undesirables, as the enemy? Yes, even the children. They were considered by Himmler and his troops to be part of the "total solution," whereby even children were eliminated for fear of the eventual rise of those seeking revenge on the children of Germany. Good God, the Nazis even sent the young ones to fight the war so desperate had they become. Desperate means for desperate minds. Like fallen flowers destroying their own seeds.

The two men moved on from town to town. Although Herr

Marchant had some kind of destination in mind—he believed his family to be in the vicinity of Rotkohl—the two men wandered like lost souls amid the ruins of war. A tenuous peace, or at least a cease-fire, existed wherever they went. Cities and towns were no longer the places they used to be. It's hard to keep one's path and maintain one's identity when all of the signposts of certainty have been demolished, and so they wandered as lonely wanderers do. There was no quest, no promise of any future, just a longing. They walked and walked and walked until their feet could no longer support their bodies and their minds wandered like listless balloons on top of a pole. They were tired and hungry. They stopped and looked at each other with a blank stare. Mechanically, they trudged along. One day they saw a signpost on the road. *Hierplatz.*

The sign itself hardly clung to the post. There was a strange silence that filled this spot, which seemed to be remote from all other areas. The two men had wandered into it just by chance and weariness. They looked around without saying a word. The stillness was eerie; the remains of bombed out buildings seemed haggard, cavernous.

"There isn't much around here," said Herr Spiegel to his companion.

"No," Herr Marchant replied, "only the dead feeling of nothingness."

"Where are we?" asked Herr Spiegel. "It's as if we are standing in a dream."

"With nothing to indicate that there is any life around here it's a nightmarish feeling," his friend remarked in a detached tone of voice.

"Let's get out of here," said the Austrian.

It was at that moment that they heard a dull whimper coming from the far left corner of the building in ruins that stood closest to them. The two men stood still wondering. What had they just heard? Was it real? Was it a human sound? Or was it simply their imaginations?

Their minds had been subjected to so many things in the last several months that they had to stop and think again what their ears had just registered. They heard the sound again. This time it was a bit louder, it sounded like a lament of desperation. Both men scurried to find out where the sound came from and who was emitting it. Could there be life still clinging to this desolate spot? For sure, it wasn't the enemy, Himmler's men. Even if it was one of them, by now, surely, such a man would no longer be an enemy. Perhaps just a vestige of the Nazi regime fighting for its life. One would have to be mad to cling to a defeated idealism once everything had been lost.

There were no more enemies now, the two men told each other, at least none of the misguided ones led by such men as Himmler and his Gestapo thugs. The head was gone, Himmler was dead. How could the body parts function without the brains even if the gray matter had been putrefied for a very long time. Men like Himmler had infected the entire body politic, he'd transformed his misguided knights into enemies of the people. Enemies of the English, the French, the Poles, and the Russians, yes, but how could a fellow citizen become an enemy of his own people? It was all one big, corrupted, degenerate, worm-eating campaign to gain power and turn it into personal gain. Power over other human beings, be they real enemies or not. It was so very easy to manufacture enemies once the head decided to appropriate to itself all power over people's lives. The slightest disagreement, the least word uttered with personal freedom, the least impulse to deny a warped sense of idealism— these were enough to create an enemy in the mind of a leader who spaded the swampy earth crawling with the worms of hatred and anger and sent the decaying dirt flying into the air. Some leaders led in whatever self-directed mode best suited them and fed their monstrous appetite for power. Their followers followed. *En masse.* It was truly an exercise of control, control by the leaders' own personal stance on things, control over people's minds, control over the destiny of nations. It snowballed faster than the exercise of freedom. The ease with which it was accomplished was truly the terrifying part of the whole scheme. Twisted minds keep twisting until they have ensnared and ensorcelled passively unquestioning minds. One big ball of worms twisting in the wind. Shivers went up the spines of both men as they thought about it.

When the two men reached the far corner of the building, they saw an emaciated old man dressed in rags and holding an old tin can that he gripped anxiously and brought to his mouth every now and then. When they saw that the tin can was empty, the two fugitives were baffled. The old beggar just sat there, a bit startled himself and somewhat confused, when the two strangers started talking to him. They couldn't get any rational word out of him. Babbling, that was all, babbling. He pointed behind him and kept on whimpering.

Herr Spiegel and Herr Marchant headed in the direction he pointed to. As they approached the rear of the fallen building, they could see heads popping here and there, eyes staring at them. Suddenly, a young girl in her late teens, wearing nothing but a torn and filthy slip, no shoes, hair disheveled, her hands clasped on her breast and a ragged purse dangling from one of her stick-thin arms, began to run in their direction. The two men stopped in their tracks. Who were these people? What were they doing here?

Herr Spiegel gasped. "*Mein Gott*, it's Dante. It's purgatory, where beings on the edge of the world lie in wait for some kind of tempered bliss."

"It makes your flesh crawl," added his friend.

As the girl was approaching the two men, a man who appeared to be in his forties, head shaved, with penetrating eyes and a slight limp in his step, also came scurrying toward them. He introduced himself. "I'm Chvalkovsky," he said, his voice hoarse. "I'm a Czech from Bratisiava. I got caught in the war and the fighting and became an enemy of the German people because I happened to be here and could not find any means of running away. My papers were confiscated and I was put in jail. While there, I schemed with another prisoner and we decided to feign madness so that, at least, we would not be sent away to a slaughter camp where they treated human beings like cattle. Worse, like condemned souls. We knew that we could be put to death at any time. The regime did not look favorably on demented people, the lame, the schizophrenics, anyone born with birth defects. But my friend and I wanted to buy time. Since this was a small village, nowhere in particular, important to no one in power, my friend and I were placed in an asylum here with other undesirables."

"But how did you survive in such an institution?" asked Herr Spiegel.

"Oh, my dear sir," said Chvalkovsky the Czech, "those who were really crazy were not inside the asylum, but outside. That's where the mad ones were. It was a mad world out there once the fighting began and the Nazi regime took over everything. I knew all along that they were out to cleanse the population of those who did not fit into their scheme of things. We were not pure enough, not desired by the real and hardy *Volk*. At first, the local townspeople had pity on us. They gave us food. Some even came to visit us. But, after a while everyone turned cold and mean. They wouldn't even smile at us anymore. They even stopped giving us food. The ones who were truly demented were not only insane. Now they were starving, as well, another injury to their madness. I feigned madness, but I knew what was happening."

"What did you do?" asked the physician.

"Well, my friend and I started to scrounge. The ones in charge were no longer watching over us. One by one, they were all disappearing. We were left to ourselves. The lunatics in charge of the crazies. But we weren't so crazy. As time went along, there seemed to be a closer bond being built among us undesirables. Those who had their minds intact but were simply in the asylum on account of their physical defects struggled to help everyone survive. It was beautiful."

The Czech sat down on a stump and invited the two men to do the same. All the while, the young girl just stood there, staring at the two men who had wandered into their midst.

"She's half Russian, half Polish," Chvalkovsky explained. "Her name is Marina. Her parents were shot by the Gestapo in their own home. First they inflicted severe pain on the mother with cigarettes and the club while they tortured the father by tearing out his eyeballs and hammering metal spikes into his skull. All this while some of the soldiers repeatedly raped the little girl. Wild animals behave better than did these beings devoid of any humanity. She was only fourteen then. She went mad. Shouting and raving mad, so much so that they left her there to fend for herself. Eventually, a neighbor brought her here, thinking that at least she would have lodging and people to take care of her. Ever since then, Marina has not uttered a single word. We keep trying to dress her, but all she wants is that torn slip. Poor girl. She carries that purse as if it was the most precious thing in the world to her. No one can touch it. It's so sad, what they've done to her.

"My God," he said after a brief pause, "was this poor girl their enemy? Who is the enemy anyhow? The enemy is no one and everyone, I suppose. Does a uniform make one an enemy? When you strip people of their clothes, they all look alike. So enemies are made from within. They do evil deeds in the most sinister and insane way."

"What happened after the authorities left?" asked Herr Spiegel.

"More and more people left the village until the place was abandoned," Chvalkovsky replied. "Some didn't even bother to take their animals with them, so my friend and I and some other interned people gathered up all of the food around and began to take care of the animals. We had chickens, two goats, one cow, two horses, three pigs, and a couple of geese. Our very own farmyard. We even started our garden and produced vegetables. Our stock began to multiply and soon we had sufficient food for all of us at the asylum. We realized that we had been abandoned. Left to our own devices. And now, as you can see, *Hierplatz* is the asylum. We are the inmates, we are its sole population. The mad ones have taken over, if you want to call us that, and we, the undesirables, are now living as a small community. We all get along quite well. No one seeks power here. And there is no one to brand us undesirable."

"What are you going to do now that the war is over?" asked Herr Spiegel.

"I'd like to return home, but I don't know if there is still one for me. Where do I belong now that the enemies have killed the enemies? I dare not ally myself with the Russians. They are supposedly the liberators, but like most German folks, I don't trust them. Strange, isn't it, how allies become enemies and enemies become allies and it's forever changing things around. It's mad. Am I going to feign madness for the rest of my life just to survive? In any case, I'm going to stay here for a while until such time as I decide what to do. This is my home. Besides, my friend is buried here. We were caught stealing food and tortured by some of the villagers. They were afraid of us. They were afraid that we would contaminate them, or that the men from the asylum would rape their daughters. I heard them talking. They thought that my friend and I were lunatics and didn't understand their talk." He chuckled bitterly, then went on. "Well, I was battered by a big, overblown, ruddy man. He snorted like a pig. He hit me so hard that my right leg was badly shattered. As for my friend, they punched him, slapped him, and slammed him into walls so wildly that he began to bleed from his nose and his mouth. Even his eyes. When they saw what they had done, they left us there and disappeared. Thanks to this frail old creature who came to check on us, she went for help at the asylum and we were brought here by some of the men. Unfortunately, my friend did not survive the beating. We had a burial for him. It was touching, the way all of these people came to grieve with me. I felt true sentiments being expressed in so many different ways. They were genuine feelings expressed the way undesirables can best express them because they not only sense loss but have lived it for so long. How can I abandon them now?"

The two strangers to *Hierplatz* sat without uttering a single word. Then Herr Marchant said in a very soft voice, choking back the tears, 'This is where true friendship lives. The regime might have classified all of you as undesirables, but you are now living the most desirable experience in anyone's life. Experiences such as this one force me to re-evaluate my feelings about other people, about myself. Especially about my country. It's not dead. It's not worm-eaten to the core. There is still some element of humanity left."

Herr Spiegel kept shaking his head in approval. Suddenly the girl approached him and looked at him intensely, as if she were seeing an apparition. She opened her mouth and faintly uttered one word, "*Otets.*"

"She's saying *father*," Chvalkovsky cried out.

The girl then took her purse in her hands, opened it, and revealed its content to the awed Herr Spiegel.

"What is it?" asked his companion.

"Why, it's a bright pink satin bow," replied the Austrian.

The two men stayed one night at *Hierplatz* and then began their wandering again, stopping here and there whenever the feeling of settling down for a while came over them. Eventually they reached Bamberg.

Bamberg was a cathedral city, the city of the Rider. The Rider rode on his horse and horse and rider were on a tall pedestal inside the church. The Rider, an unknown knight, was the great pride of the city. The pedestal had an especially remarkable carving on its upper left corner. An acanthus leaf Green Man who acts as a console to the ledge carrying the Rider of Bamberg, a beautiful work of masterful carving.

"Its a mask," Herr Spiegel said to his friend, "a human face out of whose orifices sprout leaves. A *Blatte Maske*, the finest of its kind. What it is doing in a gothic cathedral, no one really knows. No one knows the rider's identity either. It's a marvelous mystery, a syncretic blending of ancient pagan myth and Christian symbolism," he said with authority. Herr Spiegel was now in his element. He relished art and music. He thrived on them.

"Why don't you pursue your dreams?" asked Herr Marchant. "The war has certainly not destroyed art and music. They will live on forever as long as there are human beings searching for some kind of *raison d'être*."

"I think," said Herr Spiegel, 'that I will leave you here right in Bamberg and go back to my area, my roots and my arts. I now believe I can put my life together again that way. That's where I belong, in my music and my esthetics."

"There can be no better place for you," replied the physician. The two men stayed together in Bamberg for several days before they decided to part ways. Before Her Marchant left, they decided to have a party to celebrate their new future. It wasn't much of a future right now, they agreed, but things were looking up, what with the prospect of building it and making sure that the worms of war would not gnaw at it. They went to a small bar, where they joined a group of people celebrating for the sake of celebration, they said. Herr Marchant had the dark frothy beer while Herr Spiegel preferred brandy.

"Warms your soul," said he as its effects began to be reflected in his eyes. He waxed nostalgic and artistic. They were sitting alone in a corner of the bar since the others were belting out popular songs. Herr Spiegel's passion for music became unleashed as when the mountain snows accumulated during the long winter months suddenly begin to melt and their waters flow until they reach a torrential fervor.

Herr Marchant simply listened. He knew that his friend was not so much unburdening himself as restoring lost energy. The Austrian talked about Mozart with a light in his eyes that glittered like sparklers in a child's hand. "Mozart knows how to be human," he said. "He also knows how to render others fully human. He's the master of balance and harmony between sense and sensibility, between the towering vigor and inveigling certitude of reason and the lush but capricious meandering of feelings. Take his Piano Concerto No. 23. What a sublime piece, where one can actually feel the combined lyricism and grace of the piano notes interwoven with the luster of violins and wind instruments. And his violin concerti! What a harmonious whole within a unit of strains that unifies mind and heart! There is no sentimentality nor is there any plunge into barren intellect. Music just flows ... like the blood flows. It regenerates the conduits of the soul. Mozart, for me, is the very best of earth's creation in delivering to all of us the pure sense of creativity. And do you know what? Mozart heals. I can feel it under my skin, in my bones and in the very fiber of what makes me a human being. And those bastards wanted to strip us of all of this. Well, they didn't succeed. Nor will they ever succeed. You know why? The force of sublime music such as Mozart's cannot ever be stripped from our lives because it's the very essence by which we endure. Himmler and his dragon slayers never understood that."

Herr Marchant took it upon himself to remind his friend that there were other important musicians, too, such as Beethoven, Haydn, Bach, Chopin and many others. His two favorites, he said, were Débussy and Verdi.

"But they are not in the same league as Mozart," insisted the

Austrian. "Mozart towers above them head and shoulders. What is so great about Mozart is that he brings one to the threshold of the sacred, *le seuil du sacré,* as Pierre Chabanel so aptly put it. D'you remember our long conversations with Pierre on his farm in Switzerland? Mozart lifts us up mind, body, and spirit to levels of humanity rarely attained. We are raised to the spheres beyond this solid flesh, spheres where we are given to taste what it is to be whole as a human being. We are part soil, yes, but we are also part stars. What better way to soar than with music! Ah, yes, my dear friend, with Mozart—pure harmony with a sense of the sacred. It has nothing to do with religion, this sacredness, although most religions borrow this harmony touching the sacred from music."

"I realize," said Herr Marchant, "that you are carried away by your love of Mozart, but Mozart's music is not the only source of inspiration and harmony. It seems that you attribute to him the powers of the divine. No human being has yet attained perfection."

"All I know," Herr Spiegel replied, "is that Mozart's music is sublime and rarely has one attained his heights in music. They may have come close, but never equaled him. That's all I have to say."

Herr Marchant nodded his head and smiled. He was indeed happy that his friend had finally opened his heart and let things out. The war had sewn up his heart and soul until they were about to wither away, and the poor man had not been able to fully live his own level of deep humanity.

Around midnight, when people started to leave, the two men walked out and started reminiscing about their long journey together. How they had met and bonded without any mistrust and then taken the long road to Holland and then back to Germany. As they crossed the street and walked into an open road, they could see flares in the distance. The war was really not over yet. There was still some shooting, some killing and now, looting as well. Herr Marchant stooped down to pick up something on the road, a shiny insignificant thing. He heard the thump of a body falling next to him. His friend, Herr Spiegel, had fallen to the ground, a single stray bullet had pierced his brain and he had died instantly. Dead on an open road in the middle of nowhere. An untimely death, an unfortunate death, an irrational end. There was no meaning to it, at least none that Herr Marchant could attach to it. Herr Spiegel was yet another casualty of war. A homeless, landless wanderer killed for nothing. Just because he happened to be there in the line of the bullet. Dead for no purpose other than being on the margin of the war.

Herr Marchant knelt there in the road, crouched over his friend's body gently cradling the head, two burning tears falling down his weary cheeks. He knelt there like that for a long time until someone pedaling a bicycle stopped and offered a hand. The next morning they buried Herr Spiegel in Bamberg in a small cemetery not far from the cathedral. Before leaving the grave site, Herr Marchant picked up a small smooth stone and deposited it on the fresh mound of dirt that covered the dead man. He placed it reverently and silently, and then he turned around and walked toward the main doors of the cathedral. He went to the Rider, where he gently and admiringly touched the leaves of the Green Man, feeling the texture of the carving. He looked into the eyes of the Green Man. They were not wild; the look was guarded, watching and going deep inside of whoever stared at him. They were the eyes of nature looking into the eyes of man. When the irrational occurs as in time of war, nature reminds us of our rational place in the universe, and art is a mode of seeing that does not warp things but breathes life back into them.

"That's what my dear friend saw in this Green Man," muttered Herr Marchant to himself. *"Auf Wiedersehen*, my wandering friend. Wander no more ... Amadeus." And with that said, Herr Marchant turned around and walked out of the cathedral.

The people of the village of Rotkohl wondered for a while what had been going on with Sophie and her land, but eventually they stopped talking about her. She had gone away. That was all. And the land was being taken care of. In the meantime, the talk was about how someone had discovered the body of Helmut hanging from a piano wire in the square. No one knew how it got there. It was horrible, they said, horrible how this poor man, driven out by malicious tongues and abandoned by the Burgermeister and his cronies, horrible how he had been turned into an undesirable and eventually killed. Others muttered their discontent with the whole matter, citing the many strange things about Helmut, such as his gypsy look, his ways of doing things, even his lameness. "He certainly was not one of ours," they said. They realized that now.

The mother avoided the village square altogether. She said that Helmut hadn't deserved to die that way and that someone should do something about it, at least give the poor soul a decent burial, she said. The following morning, the body disappeared from the square. Mercifully, someone had taken the trouble to bury Helmut. Two men of the village spoke quietly to the mother and asked her to please allow them to bury the body somewhere on the farm at dawn so that the snooping villagers would not know where the burial had taken place. Helmut was thus buried near the wall of stones in the meadow. An unmarked grave, but close enough to the wall that it served as his tombstone. It wasn't a wall that separated, but a wall that wound its way through people's lives and land. It was not a very high wall, standing only knee high, and it was made of smooth stones, many of them worn out over the years. Other stones still had rough edges as if they had been freshly dug up from the soil or had fallen from higher ridges. The smooth stones were silent stones from the deep and solemn silence that lingered on in the meadow and settled with full rapture in the evening hours. At night, when the moon and the stars came out and the heavens seemed to whisper through the branches of the great oak tree, the wall of smooth stones captured patches of moonlight that shone like huge tallow candles burning patiently in the night.

Young lovers had spent hours on the wall of stones before the war broke out. Now young ladies sat there alone from time to time, reading letters and sometimes shedding a tear or two. Children played there, too, running all along the wall of stones. A favorite game of theirs was for two runners, one on each side of the wall, to run as fast as they could and meet at the edge of the forest where the wall ended. Then they would walk back together arms over shoulders, since they had not run for victory but for fun. The wall of smooth stones, a mute testimony of people's lives in a secluded valley where daily occurrences such as the baking of bread and the exchange of news in the town square continued for years on end. Babies were born and old people died, but the pace of life continued pretty much the same. The war claimed many lives of those conscripted for duty, and the villagers waited for their return patiently and silently. Every happening was part of daily life in the village, much as the grains of gravel and the pebbles are part of a beaten road. And the wall of smooth stones stood there as it had always done for countless years. Old stones, smooth stones, stones encrusted with lichen, round stones, flat stones, gray stones, brown stones, stones of all dimensions and all speckled shades and shapes. Farmers and landowners would keep adding stones to the wall, mending it, building it up, thus ever keeping alive the past as well as the present of the winding wall of stones.

It was mid-May and the wild flowers in the meadow were at their peak. The meadow was color-washed with yellows, blues, and bright reds. The oak tree stood there as mighty and strong as ever. The mother was doing the washing while Morgen was cleaning the barn. Suddenly, Jenny's voice called out, "There's a man coming across the hill."

Both mother and son stood frozen. Could he be bringing trouble? God knows how much trouble they already had. Who was this man? They could not make out who this stranger was until he was close enough that the mother recognized her husband, Herr Marchant. She started running toward him and screamed in such a way that one could not make out if it was out of delight or sorrow. It was her very heart that was coming out of her throat, a muffled pain finally released. The children did not recognize him, of course, but they soon got to know and love the man who was their father. They talked to him and listened to his tales long into the night. A few days later, the father told his wife that his new life was to be a farmer, a man of the land. He was going to start plowing the entire field and sow the seeds for a new harvest.

"But not the fallow side of the field, Lukas," she said. 'That part of the soil needs to remain fallow so that its richness can return and produce a healthy harvest."

"As you wish, my dear wife, as you wish," the father responded.

And thus the family settled on the land and became part of the land since they helped to produce food and enough fruits and vegetables to be able to sell some at the market on market day. "It's time to heal," said Lukas Marchant, "time to mend the soul by working the soil."

And in the mending of the times, the Burgermeister went away, his council was removed, and the villagers who had always muttered about all of the changes they had to endure became less disgruntled when they realized that some stability was coming back to their town. But some still muttered about the price of butter and radishes.

In New England, Gérard's family was getting ready to go to an evening party. They did not need to cover up the windows with black curtains anymore. They could celebrate in the bright light as they used to. Open and bright. Things were getting back to normal, people said. Gérard complained about his high-water pants and the short length of his shirt sleeves. His mother retorted that's what happens when a child grows up. "War or no war," she said, "things keep moving. Things and nature move on. Children grow taller."

Gérard looked at her with a discontented look and begrudgingly wore his outgrown clothes. After all, he muttered, what can you do about things and nature? He looked in the mirror then and admired himself, admired his growth rather than bemoaning the shortness of his trousers and shirt-sleeves. He liked what he saw, but still he wished that his mother would let him wear the clothes he wanted. Things were often that way with mothers and sons. That's just the way they were.

EPILOGUE

The two men sitting in a Berlin bar had once been boys growing up in two distant locations from one another during a time of war. Morgen and Gérard grew up, one to be a doctor, the other a college professor. The doctor had a son who left Germany and now lives in the United States. He seldom visits Germany, but has fond memories of his native soil. After the Second World War people put the pieces back together again, but the Soviets had another dictator by the name of Stalin who was as bad as, if not worse in terms of atrocities, than the Führer. A cold war with atomic missiles kept in silos was then being waged, with both sides pointing fingers at each other. A wall was built in Berlin separating East from West. Some tried to go over that wall and they were stopped, some even killed. It was a very long wall, a hard wall made to contain people. A wall of separation. A wall of sides.

With the years the wall eventually came down. The two parts of Berlin were reunited. It wasn't easy to get back together again, but with time the people made it work. The United States and Germany are now allies. Germany has become a strong economic power. All of the Nazi symbols on the walls of the Olympic Stadium in Berlin have been removed; instead, there are bare spots on the walls where they once stood.

The younger generation hardly knows anything about the Second World War, which has become a distant memory of something that happened a long time ago. It keeps getting to be further and further away. We hardly teach about the war anymore. A mere mention is made is some textbooks. Some people even think that it's old hat, this WWII. Since then, several other wars have occurred, not world wars, perhaps, but nasty blips on the radar screen that has become our technologically advanced universe. Furthermore, we now have the ability to be "surgically clean" with our bombings, since computers do our command effortlessly and efficiently. It seems, however, that people never learn or want to learn. The past keeps receding so that the present cannot absorb it adequately, and people tend to live in the future, blurring out the past and insisting that the promise of an even brighter future is coming. That those in the past "messed it up."

The story of the two men is just a story. Other stories will come and go and the world will continue to struggle and fight its wars. Enemies will come and go. Because the old wounds never healed, old enemies will come again. Others will be torn apart by the worm of revenge that gnaws within them. Will the world ever find the way to let those who want to fight, fight among themselves and leave all of those who don't want to have any part of it alone? In peace.

You see, they don't want to be marginal enemies. But maybe if we let the children lead us for once, we might see a difference. At least, let the younger children teach us how to play together and not always choose sides. Choosing sides comes later, when adults interfere with their sense of winning. Winning is everything, the adults say. Nobody wants to be a loser; nobody wants to be on the losing side. Nobody wants to lose a war, either. Will there come a day when children will no longer be marginal enemies? If and when that day comes, it will live long in people's hearts and minds, for it will be a day that will indeed be memorable. There will be more stories. That's the day the worm will have been finally crushed.

www.ingramcontent.com/pod-product-compliance
Lightning Source LLC
Chambersburg PA
CBHW032046180726
48284CB00004B/1206